Cherry Whytock

ANGEL

disasters, diets and d-cups

Cherry Whytock lives surrounded by a field full of muddy Kentish sheep in an ancient and cobwebby house with her boxer dog, Lily, and an enormous cat, Celeste, whose fur gets stuck to Cherry's husband's city suits. She has two *gorgeous* (and soon to be fabulously famous) grown-up daughters, who come home occasionally for large meals or to get their washing done. Her favourite colour is pink (of course) and she owns more pairs of shoes than is sensible.

Cherry Whytock

ANGEL

disasters, diets and d-cups

Piccadilly Press • London

For Holly, Daisy and Tilly with love

First published in Great Britain in 2003
by Piccadilly Press Ltd.,
5 Castle Road, London NW1 8PR

A catalogue record for this book is available from the British Library

ISBN: 1 85340 762 3 (trade paperback)

1 3 5 7 9 10 8 6 4 2

Printed and bound in Great Britain by Bookmarque Ltd
Design by Judith Robertson
Cover design by Fielding Design

Set in 9/16 Interstate light

The recipes in this book were inspired by Jamie Oliver, Nigella Lawson
and the author's grandmother

chapter one

Parents, Pals, Pets and PASSION

DID I FORGET to wake up this morning? This *can't* be true. Here we are, four totally *gorgeoise* girls, just about to put on the MOST horrible, stiff-petticoated, frilly-aproned, lacy-bonneted, puff-sleeved (yes, I *did* say PUFF-SLEEVED), grotesque waitress outfits. Our evening is to be spent stomping up and down stairs with dishfuls of delicacies, which are to be served to a collection of squawking old fossils that belong to my mother's vast circle of 'terribly close' luvvie friends.

Honestly, it's not as if I even agreed to *do* this. I'm sure I never heard my mother say, 'Would you mind being a cutesy-wootsey, dahling, just for me and wearing this oh-so-sweet little waitress outfit for Mummy's party?'

I mean, I would have said no, wouldn't I? But as it is, Mercedes, Portia, Minnie and I are about to squodge ourselves into these gobsmackingly ghastly frilly things (with HATS to match, when hats are just SO last season). Well, actually, I'm the only one who's going to be squodged, as Mercedes, Portia and Minnie are all – how shall I put it? – well, TINY, slim, skinny,

keeping the bulgey
bits under control

dark colours on top
– sooo flattering

some bits are best
kept covered

my most fav.
vintage jeans

eat your heart out, leg
lengthening boots

MOI!
Angelica Cookson Potts

itsy-bitsy and I'm, um, LARGE. Yes, 'large' just about covers it, although to be quite honest, not many things do – cover it, I mean.

Things went badly wrong about two and a half years ago when I was twelve. I went to bed all innocent and sweet with my teddy bear and my picture of Brad Pitt, as you do, and suddenly during the night, BOOM! – bosoms. Not those nice, well-shaped, pert little numbers that I had hoped for, but HUMUNGOUS, great barrage balloons that started under my arms and seemed to end somewhere near my navel . . . Then the rest of my body decided it wanted to match my boobs,

2

and there I was – a great, big, walloping whale with a wobble rating of about a zillion.

I don't know why my mother has decided to have a 'drinkies' party tonight. I mean, we've done the Christmas and New Year bit and now all I want to do is to curl up in a (huge, heffalump) heap, finish my Christmas chocs and dream about seeing Adorable Adam at school on Monday. But Mother just *had* to have 'a teeny-weeny party, dahling, to round off the festivities'. How pointless is that? Especially when some of us are quite well rounded off already, thank you.

Mother used to be a model, way back in the mists of time, and she still likes to surround herself with 'like-minded people' (her words, not mine). She still looks pretty good, I suppose – she is really, REALLY thin (she married *way* above her size and I obviously have none of her genes). She has cheekbones that could cut glass and very envy-making small feet. (This is SO thoughtless of her as I could at least have borrowed her shoes since the clothes are a no-no,

often wears shades 'sunlight is Mrs Wrinkles'

'Toby of Toby and I says my hair is like a baby's!'

Prada, dahling

these won't fit me – bother

Mother

but sadly her Manolo Blahniks will never be worn by Cinderelephant here.)

When Mother, whose name is Clarissa, isn't throwing parties (why do you 'throw' a party? Is the idea to hit someone with it?), she is out shopping for Britain or having bits of herself tweaked or slapped or massaged back into some sort of order. She also spends a lot of time having 'alternative therapies' (alternative to retail therapy). These are 'a lot of old rubbish', according to Flossie, our cook. The therapies might be anything from drinking gloop made from dried-up snake and kangaroo spit to lying about having needles stuck into her.

She's always having a go at me about my heffalumping tendencies and raising her eyebrows when I tidy up the remains of the pudding. She'll eat her words (HA!) when I'm a famous foodie, cooking for celebrities. At the moment, she just can't see that there is a gorgeous me hiding in my pink padding. I'm sure she can't believe that she could possibly have given birth to anything bigger than a stick insect.

ANYWAY . . . she met Potty, my father, Hector William Cookson Potts, in court. He was doing his barrister bit, with his wig on, and she was there giving evidence for her friend Lillian who was a bunny girl. (I didn't have a clue what a bunny girl was until Flossie explained it to me. It's a woman dressed up as a rabbit, with ears and a tail and nothing much in between, who serves drinks to a man in a place called the Playboy Club, which should be called the Sadboy Club in my opinion.) Lillian did something naughty with a Russian spy and my mother had to go and say that as Lillian didn't know he was a Russian spy, what she did wasn't so terrible, was it?

4

Potty was blown over by Mother's fluttering false eyelashes, and after a whirlwind romance (she must have done a lot of fluttering), they were married.

Potty is much older than Mother. He is at least a hundred and she says she is 'nowhere *near* middle age' (but she'd better hurry up or I'm going to get there before her). I do sometimes think about how old Potty must have been when they did what they had to do to make me, i.e., IT, and my mind has to go some-where else pretty damn fast – YUCK, YUCK, YUCK!!!

old school tie

his latest pamphlet

this must be a good day – he isn't wearing his pyjamas

Stinker prefers his whisky without ice

Potty

I don't know why mother bought him these, he NEVER takes them off

My father has been called Potty (short for Cookson Potts) ever since he was at school (about ninety years ago) and now he is seriously living up to his name. He's stopped doing the barrister thing now, partly because he is so old, but also because he wanted to spend more time writing his pamphlets.

He is totally potty, but divine with it, and I always say that if you are going to have bats in the belfry you might just as well have them in the whole house.

This Christmas he sent photocopies of his bottom to all the people he doesn't like, which seems like a perfectly sensible idea to me. (I wish *I'd* sent one to Slimy Sydney, but he probably would have thought it was sexy or something sick like that and stuck it up on his wall . . . Actually, I wonder if my whole bottom would fit on the photocopier . . . ?) So far Potty's had four letters complaining about his Christmas cards and Christmas was only ten days ago.

He and Stinker often enjoy 'a little stiffener' of whisky and Twiglets together. Stinker's our dog.

He's a terrorist or a terrier or something like that. The only really good thing about Stinker is that you never hear him bark and frankly, he's the only member of my family who isn't barking. He gets terribly overexcited after their 'drinking' sessions (Potty dribbles a little of his whisky over some Twiglets, which Stinker then chomps his way through), and he tends to hurtle up and down the stairs and generally misbehave.

The most important person in the entire house is Flossie, our

always smells of baking – yummy

uses this for Syrup of Figs – yuck

Flossie

6

most divine, brilliant, fab, pink and squishy cook who looks after us all and the house and everything. She has her own flat in the basement, next to the kitchen, which is the nicest part of our home in my opinion. The kitchen is huge and always sunny and warm, even when it's raining, and it always smells of something extremely edible or of warm, clean laundry, which is almost as delish. She has a bedroom and bathroom and the fabbiest cosy sitting room, with big, soft patchwork cushions and nothing so smart that you're not allowed to sit on it.

There are doors from her sitting room out into the garden, which is quite big for Knightsbridge, and three times a week Diggory comes to make the garden look wonderful. Potty loves to help and often wears his wig *and* his gown for these gardening sessions. Stinker is terribly hot stuff at digging, but not usually in the right place.

When it is Diggory's day on, Flossie makes him custard tarts, which are his favourites, and she always puts on a clean

I used to think birds nested in here

wherever Diggory goes his spade goes too

custard tarts

Diggory

pinny. 'He's my little bit of excitment,' she says with a chortle, and I think we'll just leave it at that.

We all live in this too, too smart house in Knightsbridge, 'a stone's throw from Harrods', (although why anyone would want to throw a stone to Harrods is beyond me.) Mother, Potty, Flossie, Stinker, George and me, Angelica Cookson Potts (no hyphen – hyphens are SO not smart), better known as Angel. I live at the top of the house, in Heaven (of course) and 'cousin' George lives in a room on the half landing ... He's not really my cousin. George is Lillian's son. (Lillian is the one who used to wear rabbit's ears and do naughty things with Russian spies.) Lillian and my mother shared a flat and mother says Lillian 'was like the sister I never had'. She and her husband, Hank, live in the West Indies. They wanted George to get a 'proper edu-cation', so for some reason they sent him to school here. Ever since he was a little boy with a snotty nose and scabby knees, George has spent most of his holidays from boarding school *chez moi.*

being strong and silent – or grumpy, I'm not sure which

TURBO

TURBO?
I don't think so

George

8

George is three years older than I am and is doing his A-levels. He seems to be allowed out of school a lot now. He says it's 'study leave', whatever that means. It seems more like leaving the studying to me, but I expect he knows what he's doing. He's become all 'strong and silent' these days and does a lot of 'smouldering'. Flossie calls it 'sulking' and thinks he probably needs a jolly good dose of something to bring back his sense of humour.

All my friends seem to fancy George, which is totally weird. I mean, I know he looks better now he's got contact lenses, but he's hardly a babe magnet – a fridge magnet, maybe. I can't see why anyone would fancy George. He used to cry at the end of *Bagpuss*! But Mercedes says he is 'mysterious', and I say, 'Whatever'.

Mercedes is tall and coffee-coloured and has beautiful almond-shaped eyes and wild and exotic hair. (Why is it that people with wild and exotic hair always want it to be straight?) Her parents are just SO wealthy, it's scary. Her dad runs a huge travel business and owns hotels all over the place, and her mum, who is half Jamaican and half Spanish, designs all the oh-so-posh interiors. The only trouble is, Mercedes hardly ever sees them. They're always abroad, jet-setting all over the place, so she has to live with her grandparents. But they're really lovely, her grandparents. I just think she is so lucky to have any – mine all turned up their toes before I was born.

Mercedes is brilliant at sports and has one of those well-toned bodies that, frankly, I would kill for. She's a terrible worrier, and at the moment her major worry is having to wear braces on her teeth (and we're talking train tracks here, with

Minnie thinks a bow on top adds height

spikes her hair with goo

doing her sophisticated smile without showing her brace

not many of us can wear stripes going this way

eats like a piglet and LOOK at this tummy – so unfair

Mercedes

Me

Minnie

Portia

my most divine and wonderful friends

head-gear. GRIM – but at least she only has to wear the head-gear at night). She really shouldn't worry, even if the grotty boys do call her Metalmouth, because anyone with half a brain cell (not a boy, obviously) can see she is going to be just SO exotic and beautiful as soon as the braces have done their stuff. She also worries a lot that no one will ever want to kiss her, but I am sure she is wrong.

Portia is named after some bit of a totty in a Shakespeare play. There isn't a pound of flesh on her and she eats EVERY-THING, but I love her anyway. Her parents are both doctors (which could account for her obsession with germs). Her mother is a plastic surgeon, which I think is pretty cool (I have asked her already about liposuction, but she just laughed – shame).

Their house is really lovely and sort of shambolic. Portia has two little sisters, who she quite often has to look after while her parents are working. She's really good at science (and anything to do with germs) and she's got masses of ener-gy (from all that calorie-packed food she eats, probably), and is STICK thin. The only problem with being stick thin, accord-ing to Portia, is that a) she can't find clothes that are small enough (how sad – *not*) and b) she hasn't got any boobs yet. I keep telling her, you can't have *everything*, and snake hips are WAY better than wobbly bits. To make up for her goosebump front, Portia spikes her gingery hair, which makes her look *sooo* fab and foxy, it's amazing. She says she's spotty, but honestly, that's a lie.

Then there's little Minnie (Amelia really, but she's so small that we've always called her Minnie). Well. Minnie is just TOO pretty. She has blonde hair, a sweet face and one of those per-fect, curvy cuddly figures that the boys *all* fall for. She makes out she's a total airhead, but actually she is Brain of Britain as far as maths is concerned. She is also seriously good at art and design and can make just SUCH amazing clothes. Before Christmas she made herself a posh frock out of one of her mum's old satin curtains. It was to die for – you would never have guessed that it had once been window wear.

Minnie's got two brothers, neither of whom are any use in the boyfriend department. One is much older and is in the navy. Her little brother has been sent to boarding school – he's a bit of a handful and runs away a lot. Both Minnie's

parents are really arty. Her dad is a photographer and he has a darkroom at home. Her mother is a journalist and travels a lot so Minnie is often looking after her dad. I love their house too. It's full of books and dogs and cats and you can sit anywhere without being squawked at and told not to dirty things.

Boys all think Minnie needs looking after because she's small and blonde and curvy but Minnie is oh-so-able to look after herself and has done so since she was able to climb out of her highchair.

And finally, Adam. Adam is the Love of My Life. He's in the Upper Sixth at school. He rides a huge, throbbing, motorbike and I know he would fall passionately in love with me if only he would notice that I exist. He's got this really dark hair and the sort of eyes that seem to look right through you. Not that they would ever look through me – I mean, he'd need to have X-ray vision to get through this lot. I've been considering making major Life Changes to get Adam to notice me, but I haven't quite worked out what they should be yet.

chapter two

Fabulous Friends and Frightful Frocks

CRUMBS. MOTHER IS squawking at us to hurry up and I still haven't dared to put any part of my body anywhere near this frock.

'Come on, Angel, try to be brave. It isn't for long – and look: we've all got them on,' soothes Portia.

All right then, here goes . . .

I peel everything off in a flash and try to keep the wobbly bits under control. Mercedes has the dress over my head, and before you can say 'Kate Moss', I'm zipped in.

'Help!' I try to say. 'I can't breathe!'

'Don't worry, it'll give,' suggests Minnie.

'Give *what*? Mouth-to-mouth resuscitation?' I say as I try hunching my shoulders to see if that frees up any breathing space. Then I try bending my knees to see if that makes the beastly thing look any longer . . . It's no good. It's too little, too tight, too short and all together TOO LATE to do anything about it.

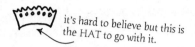
it's hard to believe but this is the HAT to go with it.

gruesome

puff sleeves, for goodness' sake

me + this = nightmare

stiff petticoats make you sound like a paper bag when you walk and are just SO scratchy

the waitress outfit

What with the hat that looks like a pair of granny's knickers and still flollops about, even with a million curby grips to keep it in place, we're like some dire sixties Motown backing group. All we need is white stilettos and some doo-wops and we'd be away.

'Thank goodness Adam can't see me now,' I gasp.

'Thank goodness *none* of the boys can see us,' says Minnie.

The rest of us don't say anything, but we are all thinking the same thing; i.e., it wouldn't matter how many boys saw Minnie looking like this, they would all *still* fall in love with her. Her curves are in all the right places, unlike mine, which are just all over the place.

There is one of those fat pauses (or is it a pregnant pause? I can never remember) while we all think about this before Mercedes says, 'Right. We might as well get this over with.' She's looking as worried as I feel . . . What if this beastly dress

15

splits and a huge wodge of me comes flopping out?

We troop downstairs to find Potty and Stinker enjoying one of their whisky and Twiglet sessions.

'How're you doing, Potty?' I ask as we rustle past in THE OUTFITS.

'Cherub!' he says. 'How wonderful to see you and your little playmates!' (He calls me Cherub because, a) a cherub is a fat angel, and b) he's stuck in a time warp.) 'What do you think – should I wear these red and white pyjama trousers,' (which he is already wearing), 'or these blue and white pyjama trousers?'

'Well, Potty, as you've got your bow tie and dinner jacket on, don't you think trousers to match might be cool?'

'Cool? Good Lord no. Don't want to be cool in the middle of winter. Got to be hip and groovy,' (that's what I mean about the time warp), 'and wear something stripy. Thought the old wig might add a touch of *je ne sais quoi* . . . what do you think, girls?'

'Super,' says Mercedes.

'Wicked,' says Portia.

'Fab,' says Minnie.

My friends really are the best. Anyone with less starch in their knickers would have run screaming from the house by now, but not these three. They understand, and that is such a comfort.

'Don't worry,' says Portia as we leave Potty to come up with his own style statement, 'my father is completely bonkers too. Just last week he came to school to collect me wearing a surgical mask because he was worried about germs. Obviously there are germs *everywhere*,' she says as she tweaks one of Stinker's hairs off her skirt, 'but to come to school in a mask??'

'Yes, but that's different,' I tell her. 'Your father's a doctor, so he's allowed to be worried about germs.' (Even though I can't imagine worrying about something as itsy-bitsy as a germ, when some of us have seriously BIG things to worry about.)

'My father wears his seventies flares because he thinks that they're back in fashion,' says Minnie. 'How embarrassing is THAT?'

'I can't remember what my father wears. I haven't seen him for so long,' says Mercedes, her face all puckered up with worry. She misses her parents so much. I think she secretly feels that they're away such a lot because they really don't love her. We all feel really bad for her, and Portia tells Mercedes that her grandparents are lovely.

'Yes, I know,' she says, 'it's just that they're so . . . sort of, well, *antique*, and they can't remember what it's like being my age. Most of the time I don't think they understand a thing I'm talking about.'

I give her a hug. Then we rustle off down to the basement.

Halfway down we can already smell that warm, almost baked, just-browning-nicely smell which is like poetry to my nose.

We find Flossie in the kitchen, crisping up the cheese aigrettes and warming the fairy-sized pizzas.

'Lawks! Just look at you four all done up like a dog's dinner!' Never one to mince her words, our Flossie.

Flossie and I have spent all day making little yummy scrummy bits for Mother's party. Cheesy things, crunchy things, crumbly things, dippy things . . . We scoured our copies of *The*

17

Naked Chef (be still my beating heart. Quite honestly, if I thought there was a chance that Jamie O would abandon Jools and run away with me I MIGHT have to put off riding into the sunset with Adam until a later date . . . oooh!) and ordered all the ingredients from Harrods. Then we mixed and whisked, creamed and blended, rolled and tasted (lots of 'tasted'), until we had produced a symphony of scrumptiousness. I know I'm getting all poetic here, but I can't help it – I just LOVE food!

It's so comforting to open the fridge door and see all those mouth-watering yummies, just waiting to be nibbled. And I love nothing more than watching Jamie Oliver, Naked Chef, with his big smile and his spiky hair, making fantastic meals to share with his beautiful friends. Food never ignores you or makes you feel guilty or raises its eyebrows at you or argues with you. It just makes you feel warm and full and happy. As Minnie might say, with her little maths mind humming, FRIEND + FOOD = HAPPY.

'What's she gone and made you wear those ridiculous frocks for anyway?' Flossie asks. 'I hope you're all going to have something smarter to wear at this fashion show of yours. At the moment you look like something out of a *Carry On* film. Still, I suppose you *will* be "carrying on", won't you, with all those trays of food up and down stairs . . . ?'

While Flossie 'carries on', we all pause and gulp a bit. Thinking about the Fashion Show next term is the last thing we need right now when we're just about to fling ourselves at the mercy of that lot of crinkly crumblies upstairs.

'Stop it, Flossie,' I say. 'We're all feeling wobbly enough

without you making it worse – although this dress is so tight, I can't wobble at all.'

Flossie chortles. I do love it when she chortles. Her cheeks go all pink, tears start to twinkle in the corners of her eyes and her whole body sort of vibrates.

'Sorry, ducks,' she says. 'You all look very much the part, I must say.' Which is one of those statements that doesn't really mean anything, but somehow makes you feel better anyway.

'Have a little try of one of these' she offers. She passes around tiny choux pastry puffs with gorgeous creamy herb cheese inside. EXQUISITE.

When we have savoured samples from every tray, Flossie tells us to stop standing around like 'a lot of spare parts', so we begin to pile the food on to the plates to take upstairs.

We do our best to make the dishes look just like something out of J.O.N.C.'s books (the thought of him saying 'pukka' in that way he has just makes me SO love him), and we're just about to start hauling them upstairs when we hear a blood chilling shriek from above.

We bound up the stairs, à la Charlie's Angels (plus one extra lumpy one), to find Mother staring at her impossibly high Manolo Blahniks. Good old Stinker had peed into one of them.

Dead Sophisticated Tiny Choux Pastry Puffs With Cream Cheese Filling

PASTRY	FILLING
60g plain flour	herby creamy cheese
50g butter	
150ml water	
2 eggs, beaten	

Heat oven to 200°C. Grease a baking sheet, then dampen it by holding it under the cold water tap for a few seconds.

Sift the flour on to a piece of grease-proof paper. Cut the butter up into little bits and put it in a saucepan with the water. When the butter has melted and the mixture begins to boil, take it off the heat and pour all the flour into it in one go. Beat the mixture with a wooden spoon until it is smooth and gloopy and comes away easily from the sides of the saucepan. Allow it to cool for a few minutes then pour in the beaten egg, a little at a time, and stir the mixture to make a thick, shiny paste.

Put tiny teaspoonfuls of the mixture on to the baking sheet and pop it into the oven for 10 minutes. Turn the heat up to 220°C and bake for another 15 minutes before peeping in at them. When they are little golden puffs, take them out of the oven and put them on a wire rack to cool. Make a hole in the side of each one with a knife to let the steam out.

When they are completely cold, cut them open gently and fill them with yummy, scrummy, creamy, herby cheese. FAB.

chapter three

Commenting Crinklies

WE FIND MOTHER another pair of unsoggy Blahniks to match her Armani cocktail dress. She mutters a lot of very rude things at Stinker before she feels ready to be the oh-so-gracious hostess and greet the first of her guests.

We go back into the kitchen to fetch the food platters. Minnie asks me to help as she struggles under the weight of half a tonne of caviar (which is one of the very few things that I think tastes completely DISGUSTING). We climb up and down the stairs, piling ourselves up with goodies, and placing them in strategic spots in the drawing room for the old relics.

I've never understood why it's called a drawing room, as if you might do arty things in it. Mother won't let me do anything more daring than draw breath in here. It's all '*eau de nil*', what-ever that means, and 'neutral tones'. The carpet is so deep that anyone smaller that Minnie might get lost in it. In fact, Stinker almost has to jump up and down just to be seen.

The sofas are covered in palest velvet and I'm hardly allowed to get near them, let alone plonk my ample bottom on the cushions, in case I squash the pile. There are antiquy things around the edges, piecrust tables (not as delish as they sound) and Mother's desk and little spindly chairs that no one should risk sitting on. (I'm not sure about antiques. Frankly, I'd rather have Ikea furniture any day.) There are a few fusty old portraits on the walls, including one of my great-great-grand-father, who was Scots. He's got an ENORMOUS face with a big pink nose and lots of whiskers. Until recently, I thought he must be on Potty's side of the family, but apparently he's Mother's great-grandfather, so maybe my huge genes *do* come from Mother's relations after all.

The guests have all arrived now and we're just beginning to totter downstairs again for re-fills when Mercedes asks, all indignant, 'Did you hear what that drippy man with the floppy hair and the sad green suit said about me?'

'No,' we chorus.

'He said that I reminded him of a young Naomi Campbell and that I just need to be "tamed". What did he mean *tamed* - as if I'm some circus animal?'

'You think that's bad?' chirped Portia. 'One old baggage told me I ought to take royal jelly, whatever that is - and it sounds like a load of bacteria to me - because it would give me a glow. I know she was looking at my spots and anyway, I don't want to glow. I'm not a worm!'

My lovely friends should consider themselves lucky. I have had nothing but people saying, 'My, how you've grown,' while they look at my chest and, 'Aren't you well developed?' while they look at my chest and, 'How did little Clarissa manage to have such a BIG girl?' while they look at my chest. And the more I hunch my shoulders to try and hide the beastly boulders, the more my mother whispers at me to 'Stand up straight and breathe in!'

Portia says she would kill to have boobs like mine. I have explained to her that I could kill WITH them. I could smother someone at five paces, to say nothing of knocking myself out when I run (not that I ever really do run – it's just SO unlady-like). I wish I could give some of them away to Portia. And Flossie always tells me I should be happy to be fit and have all my bits in the right places. But my bits are all over the place, so how do I know which ones are right?

Once the party is in full swing, Potty and Stinker make their entrance. Potty has opted for the red pyjama trousers and has matched them with a large red bow, which he found on a Christmas present and has tied around his head.

'Hail fellows, well met!' he bellows, before settling himself comfortably on the floor and nodding off.

No one really takes much notice. Mother has long ago realised that there is very little point apologising for him, and anyway she thinks it's rather distinguished to have such an 'unusual' husband. So, after this little outburst, she carries on as if nothing has happened and the guests just step over or

snoring gently

Potty in party mode

around Potty if he is in between them and where they are going.

I glance over at Stinker. He's looking a bit wild-eyed now as if he's got some master plan. 'Take cover,' I say to Minnie, 'I think Stinker is about to launch an attack!'

We stand back and wait while Stinker stalks around the room, looking for a target. Then he crouches, he leaps, he STRIKES!

'Crikey!' I gasp when he attaches his vice-like teeth to the hem of some well-lifted old bat's designer frock. Mercedes lets out a snort and Minnie giggles so much that some of the nibbly bits fall off her plate.

bet this didn't come from Claire's Accessories

old bat trying to pretend that Stinker is the ultimate fashion statement

you've got to admire him, he never gives up

'Oh my God!' says Portia, clutching her stomach as she contains her laughter. 'I totally have to pee!' Then she scuttles off before there is another disaster.

Mercedes, Minnie and I watch with our gobs completely smacked as the old bat grabs a handful of her dress and, without looking back, proceeds to sail round the room dragging Stinker behind her.

Mercedes giggles. 'She's pretending he's a fashion accessory!'

But without knowing it, Minnie has saved the day. Stinker has to decide whether to stay clamped to the diamante studded hem of his choice or eat the biscuits that Minnie has dropped on to Mother's previously pristine carpet. The biscuits finally win and he lets go so suddenly that the well-lifted old bat shoots forward, trips over Potty and lands in a very unladylike heap at the bottom of the Christmas tree.

A little voice said, 'Oooh look! The Christmas fairy's fallen off her branch.' And I PROMISE you, it wasn't me!

chapter four

Death by Dress

IT'S ABOUT TEN o'clock and there are only a few old stringy stragglers left and I know that I HAVE to get out of this vile dress and breathe properly again or I shall pass out. So we take ourselves off to find Flossie who we know awaits us with comfy clothes and FOOD.

'Honestly,' I say as we rustle down the stairs for the last time, 'who do all those old crinklies think they are, making comments about beautiful *us*? I mean, look at them, they are all Botoxed stiff and half of them have had more lifts than a fireman so their eyes won't even shut properly. And that old bag with the sunglasses and a diamond in her nose – you could just tell that she had had the fat from her bum injected into her lips.'

'So, she was literally talking out of her bottom, then?' says Mercedes.

I laugh. 'Exactly. None of them would know gorgeous if it got up and bit them!'

'But they'll all be completely awestruck when we become

models of the moment next term,' says Portia as she practises her hip thrusting model walk down the stairs.

'Oh please!' squeaks Minnie. 'Don't remind me about the Fashion Show. 'I've been sewing all through the hols, and I've still got MASSES to do.'

Last term, Mrs Worhause (pronounced War Horse), our form tutor, organised the more intelligent of us (i.e., girls) into a committee and we discussed what we might do to raise money for charity. The only things I could think of were to do with food (natch), but the others didn't think that *just* doing food was going to be enough of an event. Then a light bulb flicked on over Minnie's head and she said, 'Why don't we have a fashion show? . . . We could borrow some clothes from local shops . . . We could *make* clothes! Perhaps we could even borrow some of our parents' vintage sixties and seventies things . . .' She got so excited that she convinced us all it was a brilliant idea.

I thought we should do dinner as well. (It's not that I'm always thinking of my stomach, it's just that I do LOVE food.) The others agreed. Four girls are making fantastic posters to put up outside the school and we all have to try and sell as many tickets as possible for our Fashion Show With Fabulous Food.

When we were planning it all, we were so flushed with success at our fantastic idea that we forgot to include all the dumb animals (boys) as well. We finally decided that they would have to organise all the lighting and the music. Some of the more muscley boys in our year said they would build the catwalk. We reluctantly agreed that there would have to be boy models as well as girls (shame).

I was thrilled skinny (I wish) when the committee assigned

27

me the task of organising and preparing the food. Unfortunately I was also given the job of hostess, which means I have to prance around in a friendly sort of way, show guests to their seats and make sure everything is running smoothly.

'I really don't want to model,' sighs Mercedes. 'I can't look modelly with a mouthful of metal.' She looks so worried that I have to give her a hug and tell her that she'll look wonderful and that I'll make the world's most scrummy food and we'll all be totally famous.

Portia is going to be a model too. She's just SO this season, with her spiky hair and her 'little boy' figure. I wonder what it feels like to be as light as a feather?

'You should be a model,' says Portia.

'Don't be completely daft, Portia,' I squeak. 'The only thing I can model is play dough, and I can't even do that very well.'

'Well, I think it's a shame,' says Mercedes. 'I don't see why *you* should get away with not looking a twit.'

I consider explaining to her that looking a twit is my best thing and that I do it all the time, but thinking about the Fashion Show has got me thinking about school again. Which has made me think about Adam, which has made me think about How to Get Adam to Notice Me . . . Perhaps if I lay groaning in front of his motorbike he might think he's run me over and rush to my side and cradle me in his strong, tanned arms . . . I bet if I was the skinny little waif that Mother would like me to be he would have whooshed me away on his bike by now and we would be riding off into the sunset with our black leathers gleaming . . .

'Gawd!' says Flossie, ruining my fantasy. 'What do you look like, Angel, with your mouth hanging open like a coal shute?'

I shut my mouth quickly and realise that I'm standing in the middle of the kitchen floor.

'Let me out of here, someone!' I gasp. 'I think my vital organs are all squashed into the shape of this dress by now.' Flossie has put our comfortable clothes in her bedroom so, at last, I can be released from THE FROCK.

'Hang on, Angel,' says Portia. 'The zip seems to be stuck – there might be a bit of dirt caught in it.'

'It can't be stuck!' I wail. 'What if I have to wear this gruesome thing FOREVER? . . . We've got school on Monday. What will everyone say if I turn up for registration in THIS? And what if Adam sees me? He'll never believe that I'm his love goddess if I'm wearing a stiff petticoat and an apron!'

'He might think you are a domestic goddess,' suggests Mercedes.

'I expect they'll think you're doing it for a dare, and very brave they'll think you are too!' says Flossie, trying to reassure me.

'Flossie, please! Someone will have to get the scissors and cut me out.'

Minnie points out that the costumes are hired and Mother would go APE POO if we spoiled them.

'If only you had made them, Minnie,' I whine. 'The beastly thing would at least have fitted then.' Secretly, I'm thinking Mother has deliberately ordered my costume two sizes too small. Maybe she's trying to will me into a Size 14. She can't bear to admit that she's given birth to an elephant.

29

Mercedes tells us all to keep calm and stop worrying, which is just *great* coming from her – she could worry for Britain. 'I think it's just that you've got into a flap, Angel. Take a few deep breaths and we'll try again.'

'I can't do deep breaths. That's the whole problem.' I imagine myself months from now sitting on a beach on my summer holiday, wearing Factor 15 and this ghastly dress. At least I can take the granny's knickers off my head, so I do that and fling them dramatically across the room. They sail through into the kitchen and land gracefully in a bowl of whipped cream.

'Now look what you've done, Angel,' grumbles Flossie. 'I shall have to wash that nice little hat now.'

'Who cares about the little hat?' I squawk. 'What about me?' All right, so I am getting seriously grumpy now. I don't often throw my toys out of the pram, but HONESTLY, this is the pits.

Everyone has a go at it but the beastly thing still won't budge. Flossie comes back in just as my friends give up. 'Let me see if I can't sort this out. What we need is a little dab of butter on the zip . . .' She dabs, she tweaks, she unzips . . .

I heave a huge sigh of relief. 'This has to be the closest thing to bliss I have *ever* known.' (Apart from the time when I thought Adam was looking at me as I walked sexily across the playing fields, only to discover that he was watching the football match going on behind me.) There are a few strange red marks in funny places around my body, but that is a small price to pay for FREEDOM.

Once we are comfortably in our own clothes and Flossie has taken away the offending frocks – never to be seen again (which is too soon), we move back into the kitchen to find

Diggory sitting at the table tucking into a custard tart. What he's doing here in the middle of the night is anybody's guess, but Flossie doesn't seem to be surprised at all.

Flossie makes us all a 'nice cup of tea' and we settle down to munch our way through the leftovers and a few things that Flossie and I set aside because they were just too good for the party. Portia is tucking into her second plateful when there are footsteps on the stairs and George appears.

Flossie doing her thing with the butter

Flossie's Famous Custard Tart

PASTRY	FILLING
(enough to line a 20-cm	*3 eggs*
diameter pie dish)	*1 extra egg yolk*
120g plain flour	*2 tbsp of vanilla sugar*
30g icing sugar	*(sugar that has been stored*
80g butter	*with a vanilla pod in the*
1 egg (separate the yolk	*jar – can use ordinary*
from the white and save both	*castor sugar and a few*
in separate bowls)	*drops of vanilla*
½ teaspoon of vanilla	*extract instead)*
extract	*300ml single cream*
	150ml milk
	freshly grated nutmeg (or
	ground nutmeg)

To make the pastry, sieve the flour and icing sugar together into a bowl, cut the butter into little cubes and add it to the flour and icing sugar. Put the bowl into the freezer for 10 minutes. While this is chilling, beat together the egg yolk, vanilla extract and a tablespoon of very cold water with a tiny pinch of salt. Put this bowl in the fridge. After 10 minutes, put the flour, sugar and butter mixture into a food processor and 'pulse' until the mixture looks like breadcrumbs. Add the egg yolk and 'pulse' for a few seconds more. Turn the mixture out on to a sheet of cling film and squidge it together into a ball with your fingers. Then wrap the pastry in the cling film and put in the fridge for 20 minutes. (Boring, I know, but it falls apart if you don't.)

Heat the oven to 200°C. Dust your work surface with flour. Take the pastry blob out of the fridge and roll it out into a disc shape, slightly bigger than the pie dish. Line the pie dish with the pastry, then bake it 'blind' (this means without the filling) for 20 minutes. To stop the pastry bubbling up in the middle, put a sheet of grease-proof paper on top and weigh it down with either ceramic baking beans or any dried pulses. After 20 minutes take the pie dish out of the oven and take out the paper and beans. Beat the egg white lightly and, using a pastry brush or a very clean paint brush, brush the bottom and sides of the cooled pastry with the egg white – this helps to seal any little cracks in the pastry. Then pop it back into the oven for 5 minutes.

To make the filling, put the eggs, extra egg yolk and sugar in a bowl and whisk them all together. Warm the cream and milk in a saucepan and pour into the egg and sugar mixture. Stir and then pour through a sieve into the pastry case. Grate a little nutmeg over the top. You have to be really, really careful putting the pie back into the oven so that the filling doesn't spill. It can help to put the pie dish on to a baking tray before filling it – that way it is easier to pick up. When it's safely in the oven, leave it to cook for 40 minutes, then have a look at it. If the custard is ready it will look solid and faintly brown. Give it a little prod with your finger, just to test that it is set. If it isn't give it 5 more minutes in the oven.

This is a very complicated recipe and I can only manage it if Flossie helps me. Flossie, on the other hand, makes it 'just like that' in the twinkle of an eye and Diggory eats it just as quickly!

chapter five

Georgie, Porgie, Pudding and Pie

MINNIE HAS GONE all pink at the sight of George and even Portia and Mercedes are looking a bit goggle-eyed. What do they see in him?

He sits down at the kitchen table with us and gives everyone one of his rare, dimpled smiles. Minnie starts fluttering,

look at them all! they're drooling

George is much too busy munching to notice the gorgeous girlies eyelashes going full tilt. I shall have to talk seriously to her about this later.

Once we all get over the shock of George's arrival and he's scoffed down a few golden, crumbly, sausage rolls (while my three friends stare at him and do a sort of multiple drooling act – which has nothing to do with the sausage rolls), we can relax again and, to the sound of Stinker happily chewing on someone's forgotten evening bag, begin to discuss Life.

Stinker kindly customising someone's evening bag

This term, Life is going to be all about the Fashion Show With Fabulous Food and deciding which GCSEs to take. Obviously anything to do with school is deeply yawn-making, but these things just have to be faced. Choosing which subjects to take means having to think about What You Want to Do When You Leave School, and here, I have to admit, I do feel just a teensy bit smug.

Ever since I first saw Mr J Oliver, Naked Chef extraordinaire on the telly, I KNEW I had to *be* him. Well, not be him exactly as he's a bloke (be STILL my beating heart) but I knew I wanted to do just what he does – COOK. I mean, I just love it (and him) and I can't think of anything more wonderful than making yumptious scrumptious 'pukka' food for people and watching them eat it.

Of course, Mother thinks cooking is something that only the lowest of the low do. She just doesn't understand. I mean, she's never once eaten a whole meal with pudding (and cream), so how *could* she understand? I expect she thinks being a fashion stylist or a beautician would be much more the sort of thing *her* daughter would do. Flossie can't believe my mother doesn't know how to boil an egg. 'It's not natural. How would she manage on a desert island? I'd like to know.' But actually, it probably wouldn't be lack of food that would finish her off on a desert island, but lack of lipstick.

'You are just so lucky, Angel,' says Mercedes. 'You already know what to do and your parents are always here to talk to about things.'

'Yes,' I say doubtfully, trying to remember the last time I had a sensible conversation with either of my parents. All my mother ever really thinks about is what she looks like and whether her wrinkles are getting wrinklier. As for Potty, he's SO sweet and he does mean well, but he's more likely to suggest that I become an astrophysicist than anything remotely possible.

'Seeing as I hardly ever get to see my parents, I have no one to talk to about this stuff. I'm sure I'll make all the wrong decisions and then they'll get all upset with me.' Mercedes squidges her face up just like a prune. Poor thing. She does worry so. I'm sure if my father was rich enough to buy Great Britain I wouldn't worry about anything, but I know she feels that she's been dumped on her grandparents. Being rich and skinny and beautiful doesn't seem to make up for that. I want to say that if I could be as rich and skinny and beautiful as Mercedes I would live with *anyone's* grandparents, but I decide it's probably better to keep quiet as it's probably not true anyway.

I wish I could think of something really helpful to say to her, but before I can come up with anything, George asks, 'What do you *want* to do, Mercedes?'

Mercedes looks a bit coy and says, 'I really love sport and I'm sort of good at it. Perhaps I could be a personal trainer or even teach . . .'

'SORT of good at sport!' we all snort.

'You're *brilliant* at it,' I say and turn to face George. 'She's the fastest runner the school's ever had and she's on every team and captain of most of them too!' I'm making her sound like something out of an Enid Blyton adventure story and quite honestly, all this talk about sport is making me incredibly hungry . . . Perhaps just one more tortilla roll?

'My mum and dad want me to do something arty because of my mother being such a brilliant designer,' Mercedes goes on, 'and she *has* made a really good career of it . . . but I just don't know.' Then she gets a bit tearful.

Portia, Minnie and I give her a sort of group hug and Flossie says she has got just the thing – 'a little pick-me-up' – to make Mercedes feel better. She leaves the room and comes back with a bottle and spoon in her hand. She gives Mercedes a large spoonful of something that smells suspiciously like gin, which makes her splutter, but she does manage a brace-concealing smile afterwards, so Flossie is satisfied. But really, it's not as if any amount of Flossie's mixture is going to make the situation better. How are we supposed to know NOW what we might want to do when we are really old, like twenty or something?

Realising that it's probably best not to push Mercedes any

further, George turns his attention to Portia. 'And what about you, Portia? Do you know what you want to do?' He's putting on his concerned older man act, which he no doubt thinks will have girls eating out of his hand. Depressingly, it does seem to be doing the trick.

Portia explains that she would love to be a doctor, maybe something to do with skin (she touches her face anxiously) and that both her parents are doctors – her mother is a plastic surgeon.

Minnie tossing her hair for George (for goodness' sake)

I love this top. I wish she would make one in Size Huge

'She probably knows *all* my mother's friends,' I cut in.

'Yes, well, my mother is a plastic surgeon and my dad is an oncologist . . . so I'm sort of nervous that I won't be as good as them . . .'

I don't really think Portia is nervous at all – she is so brainy it's terrifying. But for some reason my friends seem to think it's a really good idea to act dumb in front of George.

'At least *you* have a good idea what you *want* to do,' says Minnie. 'But I just haven't got a clue!' Why is she doing this hair tossing bimbo bit? 'Can you think of anything, George, that *I* could try?'

I want to scream, 'Don't do this, Minnie. He's not worth it – he used to wet his bed!'

'I haven't got a clue . . .'

Honestly, shall I remind her that at this precise moment she is wearing two items of clothing that she has designed and made herself? A hand-painted T-shirt and a beautiful beaded belt. She probably crocheted her own lacy knickers, for all I know. She just doesn't seem to realise how amazingly talented she is. She could make a fantastic career in fashion, but for some reason she doesn't think that fashion is proper work, or rather, that she would be good enough at it to make a career of it – totally bonkers!

Thankfully George doesn't seem to be listening anyway and Flossie decides it's time Minnie had something else to eat.

Mercedes and Portia are in deep conversation with George and Flossie is tending to Minnie. So I busy myself imagining I am a world-famous cook, who has a truly posh restaurant and TV shows on several channels. (Obviously I would have to be sure that the camera never shot me from behind – although, who knows? By then maybe I'll have made radical Life Changes and be paper thin with a wobble rating of zero . . . I suppose I could start jogging to school, or should that be jog-gling? But flat-soled trainers are just SO unflattering and as I said, I never run.)

I'm snapped out of my reverie when Diggory, who hasn't said a thing all evening but has ploughed his way manfully through a whole plate of custard tarts, suddenly gets up and says he ought to be going. Flossie goes with him to the door and we try not to hear the kerfuffle that goes on on the doorstep.

She comes back, pushing a strand of escaped hair behind her ear and Minnie, trying to gain George's attention, bashes on again. 'I mean, I am a tiny bit good at making clothes but I don't expect I would ever be clever enough to make a career out of it.'

'Honestly, Minnie, you are talking a pile of poo,' I say and she looks a bit deflated. 'We all know you are a major maths mastermind who happens also to be really good at making fab and cool clothes. You know, George, she's making all these amazing things for the school fashion show next term. You can just give her any old bit of stuff and she'll make something totally glam out of it.'

I don't even want to think about why Flossie's hair is in a muddle after saying 'goodbye' to Diggory . . .

'Are you going to be a model, Angel?' asks George.

'Oh yes, of *course*!' I say with HEAVY sarcasm. 'I'll look just gorgeous wobbling down the catwalk. It's bad enough that I have to be hostess as well as doing all the food. I think I'll skip the catwalk bit.'

'That's a pity,' says George. 'You'd be a *great* model.'

All the girls start nodding. I think about explaining that being *great* is my whole problem, but decide to go back to discussing Minnie instead. 'Just because you're MUCH TOO pretty, Minnie, doesn't mean you have to pretend to be a complete airhead.'

Minnie gives me one of her 'I'll *kill* you later' looks (or in her case, 'I'll grow a bit first and *then* kill you later' looks) and I know I've gone too far, so I whizz around the table to give her a kiss and say, 'I'm sorry. It's only because I'm jealous.'

She glances anxiously at George, who seems to be off in a daydream. Then he gets up and says he must go and read some Shakespeare. (Poser.) 'Don't worry, girls. GCSEs are the easy bit. It's when you have to make your A-level choices that life gets really hard.' He gives us a strong, smouldering look and says, 'Angel, all this food was fantastic, you really are a brilliant cook!'

now, if that's not the face of someone who's just a TEENSY bit cross, I don't know what is ←

I know he's only buttering me up so that I'll make him a choco-late cake to take back to school, but Minnie doesn't know this and she is making a face like a bulldog eating a wasp.

After George leaves the room, the oh-so-slightly-sticky atmosphere is relieved by the sound of Stinker sicking up sequins under the table.

We are *sort* of all friends again by midnight when the girlies call a taxi and leave. It would have been horrid to go back to school on Monday with Minnie being so cross and upset. Besides, I need all my energy to concentrate on getting Adam to notice me. I've got just one day before the beginning of term . . .

I go upstairs to run a bath and de-stress. Catching sight of myself in the bathroom mirror, I notice that my wobble factor

41

seems to be way over a zillion. Perhaps it is time to begin my Life Changes?

I try making the bath really hot, in the hope that the steam from the water might melt off some of my pink padding. But all that happens is that my entire body goes puce and sort of swells . . .

Must remember to cross 'steam bath' off my Life Changes list.

chapter six

Pass the Potatoes, Please

I WAKE UP late on Sunday morning and go to see what everyone's up to. Mother is spending the morning resting on the sofa with an eyemask on. She told Flossie she was 'emotionally drained' after her party, but I know that she had one or two 'tiny cocktails' too many. And now she is trying to de-bag her eyes with the latest skin soothing, liposome-rich, callogen-soaked hugely expensive rip-off from Horrids.

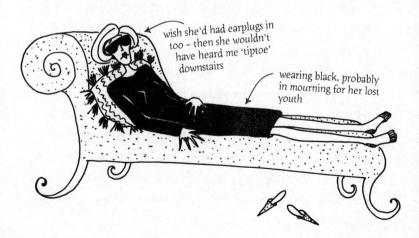

wish she'd had earplugs in too – then she wouldn't have heard me 'tiptoe' downstairs

wearing black, probably in mourning for her lost youth

The only time she bothers to speak to me at all is when she squawks at me not to 'gallumph' down the stairs 'in that ear-splitting way'. Why is she so grotty? I wasn't gallumphing – I was doing my Kylie Minogue Brit Pop Award-winning entrance. I was FLOATING down those stairs. Mother always has to have a go at me about my size, just because she's a lollipop stick.

I know she thinks that I'm a greedy guzzler. She doesn't understand that it's just that I'm really interested in food. I love all the smells and the colours and the crunchy bits and the creamy bits. It's like I'm an explorer when I'm eating, sort of discovering new things with every forkful . . . What's the use? She never takes the trouble to find out what it is I love about cooking, or even what I think about ANYTHING. I'm sure she thinks I just make the house look untidy and take up too much space. She doesn't realise how UNBELIEVABLY lucky she is to have me around! She'll never know how lovely food is now she's a dried up old sultana and it's no use trying to explain, especially when she's 'tired and emotional'.

Potty's busy writing one of his pamphlets. This one is called 'How to Embalm the Queen's Corgis' (with diagrams). He's planning to hand it out to unsuspecting tourists outside Buckingham Palace later in the week. He's very lucky – most of the police know him now and he only very occasionally gets arrested. He's never been convicted, though, because the police all realise that he's totally potty and he doesn't actually do any harm. They usually just take his pamphlets away and phone Flossie. She's quite used to collecting him and bringing him home. When they get back, she calls him a 'silly billy' and makes him 'a nice cup of tea'.

44

Stinker, bored with Potty's company, joins me as I 'gal-lumph' down to the kitchen and we both help Flossie make Sunday lunch. No, Stinker doesn't cook, but he does Hoover very nicely while we cook all this gorgeous stuff. Today's lunch is:

Fresh field mushrooms stuffed
with tomato, basil and cheese

Roast loin of pork with bay and red wine vinegar
Roasted red onions (that's one of J.O.N.C.'s – oooooh)
crispy potatoes and steamed green beans

(and the star of the show . . .)

Treacle sponge pudding with cinnamon ice cream

None of your scratching around, fridge gloop Sunday lunch here. This is the REAL THING.

We always have Sunday lunch in the dining room. (Mother insists. Still, it is just about the only meal I have to eat with her watching me.) This means 'gallumphing' up and down the stairs again with all the food. I'm not really that keen on the dining room. Apart from the 'gallumphing' aspect (I'm still really upset about this), there is Potty's collection of erotic art, which is all over the walls. I'm sure it's all very valuable and terribly interest-ing and all that stuff, but it's *sooo* embarrassing and you don't know where to look. I would rather not have a large naked bot-tom twinkling at me while I eat my roast pork, but what can I do?

George, Mother and Potty join us for lunch. Potty greets me with his usual 'How's my favourite Cherub today?' and I almost tell him that if mother 'gallumphs' at me once more, I shall run away to sea. (Actually, those sailors can be SO good-looking – maybe that's not such a bad idea . . .)

It all goes fine, with Potty and George complimenting Flossie and me on the 'pukka tukka' (there goes my beating heart again!), until Potty says that my gravy is 'heavenly'. Mother, of course, doesn't comment, then she suddenly chirps at me, 'Don't you think you've eaten quite enough potatoes, Angel?'

What does she mean, 'quite enough'? No, obviously I haven't eaten 'quite enough', or I wouldn't be eating more, would I?

I am almost choking with rage and potato and I tell her that she is always having a go at me and that I will, at any moment, be off to pack my rubber ring, leave home and join the navy. She tells me she was 'only saying it for your own good, dahling'. What good does she think it will do? It's just so unhelpful to have her remind me that she thinks I'm huge all the time. I mean, I'm very tall like Potty and just not very thin like her. I know my boobs are a bit out of control and there are some wobbly bits, but they are only puppy fat and will disappear when I stop being a puppy.

I was feeling really good when I woke up and now, with the 'gallumphing' and this potato business, she's spoiled it all. I love potatoes, and these ones are stupendously delish and it would be such a waste not to enjoy them.

George and Potty are too busy tucking in to come to my aid, but Flossie tutted when Mother mentioned the potatoes. I

delish crispy potatoes

decide to eat as many as possible, just to annoy her. When I help myself to the last three, Mother sighs loudly and I completely ignore her.

When it comes to afters, Flossie gives me an especially big slice of treacle pud and a big wink which makes me feel a bit better. I thought that I would make 'no pudding' one of my Life Changes but as soon as I saw it, all glistening and gooey, with that dollop of soft melting ice cream on top . . . well, no one could to resist that. Honestly!

Stupendously Delicious Crispy Potatoes

2 tbsp vegetable oil   plain flour

as many potatoes as you   grated parmesan cheese

think you will need

Heat the oven to 190°C and put a baking dish big enough for all the potatoes in the oven with the oil in it to get really hot.

Peel the potatoes and cut into halves or even quarters if they are really big and par-boil them. (This means putting them in boiling water for about 5 minutes.) Drain them. While they are still hot, sprinkle them with flour and parmesan cheese, making sure that they are well covered (a bit like me!!). When you are sure that the oil is hot, very carefully put the potatoes in and turn them in the oil. Roast for about 40 minutes or until you think they look deliciously crispy enough!

P.S. It's a good idea to wear an apron for this as a splash of oil on your clothes is *really* hard to get out.

chapter seven

Bike Shed Blues

UGH! I AM not a pretty sight. It's much, much too early for anyone to be ALLOWED to be awake AND it's the first day of term.

I scrub myself clean. We're not allowed to wear a *smudge* of make-up at school. Of course we *do* wear it – I mean, a girl has to be presentable, doesn't she? It's just that it can't be obvious. I put on my gorgeous, glamorous designer uniform (not) and my sensible shoes. (Honestly, who on earth wants to be sensible? And anyway, aren't my L.K. Bennett pink snakeskin stiletto boots sensible? A little

Monday morning mood

of course I look grumpy – I'm wearing PLEATS and pleats are just SO unflattering

49

glamour in the footwear department wouldn't go amiss on this grey, drizzly, grumpy January morning.)

Perhaps it's a good thing that I have to go back to school today. We've got a meeting about the Fashion Show and I can stun everyone with my tastebud-trembling food ideas. I'll see my lovely friends (and Slimy Sydney – groan) and it will mean that I can eat my lunch without my mother making me feel self-conscious . . . I wonder if Adam had a good Christmas? If I had a sprig of mistletoe in my pocket I could hang it up in the assembly hall and accidentally find myself under it as he walked past . . . I wonder what he kisses like . . . ?

Oh help! There's the doorbell and I haven't put my lip-gloss on yet.

Mrs Sophie Something-Hyphenated, who lives next door, drives me to school. Potty is not really supposed to drive any more as he tends to park at traffic lights, which can annoy other drivers. I don't think Mother knows how to drive, and even if she did, she's so neurotic we would all be nervous wrecks before she got the car out of the parking space. Flossie can drive, but she's always really busy in the

artificial flower in hair come rain or shine

boobs may be tucked into her belt

biodegradable plastic bag

recycled cardboard shoes

Mrs Sophie Something-Hyphenated

mornings. I'd rather do anything than have to go to school with Mrs Sophie Something-Hyphenated but it's too far to walk (well, I'd have to get up at about 2 a.m. to get there on time), and the buses are so full in the morning, there's never any room for a heffalump with a school bag. There are plenty of schools in the area, but Potty insisted I go to a comprehensive school. He said he wanted me to have a 'well-rounded' education. Well, I've certainly got the 'well-rounded' bit, and maybe the education is hiding in there, somewhere.

Mrs Sophie Something-Hyphenated is terribly into good works and things being eco-friendly. She drives a huge Range Rover (which Potty has pointed out is about as eco-UNfriendly as you can get). It has lots of pairs of wellies in the back (where is the mud in Knightsbridge exactly?) and smells of vomit – probably because her two small stinky children are always throwing up and having allergic reactions to things. They go to the primary school that's almost next door to our school.

small stinky child

smaller stinky child

The little Something-Hyphenateds have to be the beastliest children ever and seem to work on the idea that children should be ob-seen and always heard. They are always asking me loudly whether I've snogged anyone lately (I wish) or whether I've got my period. I mean, they are only six and eight years old! Should they know about these things?

I hate them to pieces and Mrs Sophie Something-Hyphenated never tells them to shut up because she believes in free expression or some such poo. I usually try to have some big sticky toffees in my pocket in the hopes that these will glue their little jaws together until we reach school. This morning especially I need time to think about possible Life Changes. Unless by some miracle Adam actually notices me today, in which case we'll ride off into the sunset and that will be that – I shall do something really radical so that everyone will see me for the TOTALLY *gorgeoise* me that I really am. By the Fashion Show I could definitely be SPECTACULAR!

I arrive at school. Same old grey walls, same old smell of cabbage, same old classmates . . . Still, there's always that exciting bit at the beginning of term when you have a good look around at registration and see who's had a new haircut, or who's tanned from a 'look at *moi*' Christmas holiday abroad, or who's got really spotty from too many Christmas chocs. Sometimes you catch a glimpse of a love bite which of course leads to a close interrogation later.

If I had a love bite, I would frame it with a big ring of red lipstick and make a cut out arrow to pin to my shoulder so that *no one* would miss it.

Where are my lovely friends . . . ?

I catch up with them walking along the drab corridor to our classroom, 9C. There are loads of us in Year Nine, so we've been split into five different classes. It's just amazing that we four fabulous friends have landed in the same class for the last two years.

'Hi babes,' I say, as I FLOAT towards them. 'Have I missed anything?'

'You missed Adam arriving on his dirty, polluting, motorbike and all the girls blowing kisses and waving at him,' says Portia. DAMN.

Minnie, meanwhile, looks as if she hasn't entirely swallowed that wasp from Saturday night, so I put my arm around her shoulders and apologise again for being an old cow, 'with big udders', I add, hoping to make her laugh.

'It's all right, Angel,' she responds, 'I know I was being a bit of a bimbo. It's just that I never think anyone I like is going to like me back, and George is *sooo* lovely.'

I still can't work out why anyone as clever as Minnie, who could have her pick of the boys, wants to waste her time on George, but I tell her that she doesn't need to try to make George like her – she must just be herself . . . Gosh, I sound like Flossie. But Minnie is one of those people who are just perfect as they are. In fact, all my friends could have stepped out of glossy magazines, and they are ALL so lovely with it . . . Now where did Adam go?

As I'm looking for the trail of motorbike exhaust the first bell goes and we have to get our beautiful selves to our classroom.

We can hear our classroom before we can see it. It sounds like Saturday night after a football match from out in the corridor. When we get inside we can see why. Complete chaos. The boys are standing on the desks, having a farting competition while playing volleyball with a blown-up condom. Has anyone explained to boys that they are supposed to GROW UP at some stage before their ninetieth birthdays? How can they possibly be the same age as us girls, when we are so totally sophisticated and adult?

Vivi finding a whole new use for her nail file →

We stand staring for a bit from the doorway. Some of the other girls in our class are sitting in a corner sharing a quiet moment with their make-up bags and seem to be successfully pretending that none of this is happening, until the condom bounces off Vivi's head and one of the boys shouts, 'It's a goal!'

Vivi is not usually vindictive. In fact, she's the sort of person who would do anything for anyone. I know it's mean, but we all call her Vivi the Scivvy because she seems to just love being everyone's slave. This morning it's obviously a little bit too early for her sense of humour to have woken up. She takes her Diamond Deb nail file and shoves it as hard as she can into the condom. There is an amazing bang and the boys all stop, mid-fart, to stare at Vivi. After a second or two, a voice shouts,

'She's popped our willy warmer!' (I mean, how disgusting is that?) They begin climbing off the desks and looking for something else to occupy their minds (minds?), when Sydney, having had his pathetic game spoiled, spots me in the doorway.

'Oh no!' I hiss. 'Stand in front of me, girls. The slimeball has seen me!' Of course, it's no use because I am much taller than the others, and anyway, Sydney is not that easily put off. Minnie is grinning at me – she thinks Sydney fancies me. I mean, as *if*. I don't think so. And anyway, he's so, so . . . SLIMY.

'Hi, Jelly Cooking Potts,' he says as he oozes over. 'Had a bra-filled – oops, sorry – *fun*-filled Christmas, then?'

'Yes, thank you,' I answer in my best 1940s BBC broadcasting voice, and walk past him towards an empty desk in the classroom.

'Did your cups runneth over with Christmas cheer?' (He always does the 'cups runneth over' thing.) I hunch my shoulders a bit in the hopes of disguising the 'runneth over cups'.

'I'll bet you were a bit of a handful during the holidays!' He grins, and we all know he isn't talking about my personality here. 'Nice jelly moulds, though,' he adds. CREEP!

Right. It's time to draw myself up to my full magnificent height, look sternly down my nose and make that 'What's that appalling smell?' face that my mother is so good at (and usually it's Stinker – the appalling smell, I mean) and I say, 'Sydney, you are nothing more than a pimple on the earth's bottom.'

I'm feeling pretty good about this put-down, but he is so good at finding my weak spots – or rather, my weak, wobbly spots. I do wish I didn't let them get to me in the way that they do.

He's just opening his mouth to come back with some other size-ist remark when the door is flung wide open, and in strides Scarlet in a flurry of red hair and a whiff of Miss Dior. Scarlet is the class drama queen, and for some reason the boys are all really impressed by her. They're so shallow, boys – can't they see it's all an act? Anyway, in she flounces and proceeds to tell everyone in her loud, 'Listen to me, I'm fascinating' voice that she has had 'the most AMAZING Christmas holidays . . . I was discovered by a film director while visiting *le sud de France*,'

seldom far from her sunglasses

she's done something clever to make her skirt straight

Scarlet
making an entrance

(for goodness' sake) 'and he is *definitely* going to make me a star. He thought I had the most *captivating* laugh . . .' She gives us a blast of her captivating laugh.

'Sounds like a cat being strangled,' whispers Portia.

'. . . and that he will be casting for his next movie any day now. So take a good look at me, I may not be amongst you ordinary folk much longer . . .'

She goes on a bit, but frankly the girls have all lost interest by now. She's such a freak. The boys, however, are looking like a collection of gargoyles with their mouths hanging open and their tongues lolling about. It's a pity they can't use their single brain cell to work out what a poser she is. Still, I suppose it's lucky for her that *someone* thinks she's great. She's always banging on about how amazing she is, but no one really LIKES her. Vivi acts like her slave, but I don't think she is really her friend. We ought to pity Scarlet, I suppose . . . but I can't – she is SO annoying.

While Scarlet bores on about how fantastic she is my mind wanders towards the bike shed and I begin to imagine meeting Adam there as he parks his big, red, throbbing motorbike . . . He grins at me as he takes off his helmet. I smile sweetly back whilst bending my knees a bit. (It's not that Adam's small exactly, just that he is smaller than I am.) He strides over and says, 'Angel, you look a little cold. Here, let me wrap you in my jacket,' and he takes off his leather jacket and drapes it gently around my shoulders whilst looking deep into my eyes. (I might have to bend a *little* bit further at this point, in order for our eyes to meet.) Then he brushes my cheek with his fingers before his lips . . .

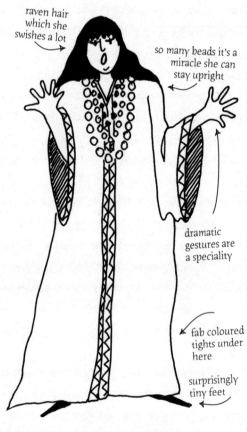

raven hair which she swishes a lot

so many beads it's a miracle she can stay upright

dramatic gestures are a speciality

fab coloured tights under here

surprisingly tiny feet

Ms Worhause

Ms Worhause has just appeared. I would just LOVE to be as wacky and confident as she is. Today she is wearing an emerald green sparkling tent thing, with all sorts of beads that look like boiled sweeties around her neck. She is utterly fab. She teaches drama and sometimes there are literally fights to get into her productions. She is large (which I like) and raven-haired, and everything about her is dramatic. When she speaks, her mouth makes the most amazing shapes so that you can't help watching.

We all scuttle to our desks. Someone has thrown away the popped condom and the boys are looking as if butter wouldn't melt – AS IF!

chapter eight

Adopt Me, Anyone?

'I HOPE YOU have all had a magnificent Christmas, and that before you all get excited about the Valentine's Day disco (my stomach does a backflip – I had COMPLETELY forgotten about the disco!) and the Fashion Show, which are undoubtedly the highlights of this term, you have given some thought to your all important Options?'

Ms Worhause shimmers and sparkles while her mouth does the lambada around these words. Sickeningly Slimy Sydney is sitting right in front of me and I watch, fascinated, as the sunlight coming through the window catches her beads and makes little coloured fairy lights appear across his left ear. I wish I could lean across and tell him what a saddo he looks.

Sydney is one of those boys you want to stick a pin into to pop their huge, inflated egos. He thinks he's SO funny and the other boys in our class treat him like he's some kind of god, just because he's really good at football. Portia thinks he's good-looking. (I can't think why – she's always telling us that she hates germs!)

Mercedes is shuffling a bit in her seat and I know she's worrying again about how to make the right GCSE descisions when she doesn't know what she wants to do with her life. I'm *sooo* lucky that I know what I want to do.

I'm just sitting at my desk, enjoying the Blackpool Illuminations on Sydney's ear and thinking about what I will wear to the Valentine disco when I hear Ms Worhause say, 'And of course I shall be discussing all this with your parents next week.'

Oh, NO! I had forgotten all about THAT too! I've been so busy thinking about the Fashion Show food and all the Life Changes I'm going to make so that Adorable Adam will fall at my feet, that I had completely blanked out the awful, awful prospect of Parents' Evening. This is some kind of daymare. My parents *here*? Discussing *me*? . . . What will Potty do? Will he bring his pamphlets? Will Mother remember who I am? How will they discuss me? My parents don't do discussions . . . They don't understand anything about me. Flossie is the only person who actually TALKS to me. Mother will probably want to talk about my size and what will Potty wear? People might SEE them . . . oh, PANIC!

I feel my breakfast (Flossie's homemade muffins with unsalted butter and strawberry jam) do a sort of break-dance in my stomach. My brow begins to glow (Mother always says only horses sweat) and I think I might be going to faint . . . I've never managed to faint yet. I've always thought it would be so *sophisticated* to crumple at someone's feet – preferably Adam's – and have him bring me round with a sip of something cooling and a dab of cologne to my temples . . .

I don't faint. But the rest of the day is spent in a fog of awfulness. I just keep imagining my parents here at school and how HORRIFIC it will be. Maybe I won't remind them (they'd never remember themselves). Maybe I'll tell Ms Worhause that they have run away to join the circus. Or that I have just discovered that I am Portia's sister and then come with her parents instead. Her parents are so nice and clever and normal. Or maybe I could find some sensible-looking people wandering around outside Harrods and ask if I could borrow them for the evening?

It's all right for Minnie – her father is a governor, which means he almost runs the school anyway. My parents don't even know their way around. I'll have to show them and therefore be *seen* with them. I'll have to try to explain to them about GCSEs and how important they are and how some will be better for a cooking career than others.

Mercedes will be coming with her grandparents, who are at least sensible even if they are a tiny bit on the ancient side. She worries that they don't understand 'modern' education. Also because her grandparents aren't coffee-coloured like her, she thinks people will imagine that she's adopted or was an abandoned baby . . . I wish sometimes that my parents would abandon me.

I get myself into such a fluff, which only gets worse as the day progresses, that the gorgeous girlies have to come home with me to make sure I'm all right (and to see if Flossie's baked anything scrumptious today).

We troop off on the bus. I take the bus home because Mrs Sophie Something-Hyphenated's odious children don't stay at

62

school as late as we do, which means I don't have to discuss sexually transmitted diseases or some such choice subject on the way home.

'Perhaps Flossie will have made some of her amazing meringues,' says Portia, hungry as always.

'How can you think about meringues when my life is so in ruins?'

'But a meringue might cheer you up.'

'The only thing that could possibly cheer me up is if I catch a fatal disease before next week,' I say, doing my best to look tragic.

'Perhaps George and I could dress up and pretend to be your parents,' says Minnie, giggling.

'You just want to play Mummies and Daddies with George . . .' I say. 'Ooops! Sorry, I didn't mean to be horrid.'

'I know.' Minnie gives my arm a squeeze. 'But actually, I wouldn't mind playing Mummies and Daddies with George,' and she giggles the little giggle that always makes the rest of us giggle too, and I begin to feel a bit less like throwing myself under the wheels of the bus.

As soon as we get into the kitchen Flossie decides that Portia is 'looking peaky'. She isn't looking peaky at all; it's just that she's skinny and Flossie is more used to seeing big, healthy me. Anyway, why hasn't she noticed that I am on the verge of a nervous breakdown? She decides that Portia must 'need a purge' and proceeds to give her a huge spoonful of Syrup of Figs.

'Ugh!' says Portia. 'That was possibly the most disgusting thing I have ever swallowed!'

the dreaded Syrup of Figs

she'd be better off making a run for it than gripping the seat . . .

'But it will sort your problem out nicely,' Flossie points out.

'No amount of Syrup of Figs could sort my problem out, Flossie,' I whine.

'Oh, I'm sure I can find a little dose of something that would be just the thing . . . Now, tell old Flossie what the problem is.'

'My parents have to come to school next week and discuss me,' I wail.

'Oh,' says Flossie, and for a moment I think I have finally flummoxed her. She blows out her cheeks and asks, 'So?'

'So? So? You know "so"! This is Mother and Potty we're talking about.'

'Come on, Angel,' Mercedes pipes up. 'Your parents are lovely.'

'They're not lovely, they're LOONY - Stinker could discuss me better than they could.'

'Well, Stinker will probably come with your parents,' Flossie ventures.

'Flossie, is that supposed to make me feel better??' I'm getting all pink around the edges now and I really think I might cry except I don't want to smudge my new super-extending, thickening, mascara.

'Now look here, young lady,' orders Flossie. (I always know I'm in for it if she calls me 'young lady'.) 'It's time you calmed yourself down and counted yourself lucky that you have two loving parents at all.'

While I'm calming and counting there's a ring at the basement door and Mrs Sophie Something-Hypenated appears, the artificial rose in her hair dripping slightly from an early evening shower.

'Flossie,' she says, 'I'm campaigning for a ban on achohol in the area and I wondered if Clarissa would be interested in being on the committee . . . ?'

This is the funniest thing that has happened all day and the three of us are unable to look at each other for fear of bursting. Flossie keeps her cool, though, and with her hands on her hips, she says that she will of course ask Mrs Cookson Potts, but she knows that she is very busy at the moment. Mrs Sophie Something-Hyphenated says thank you, and yes would she, please, because she feels sure that Clarissa would be a valuable member of her anti-alcohol campaign and that Clarissa would probably appreciate having a little outside interest. With that, she turns on her recycled car tyre wellie and leaves.

There is a short silence before we all squeal in chorus and I have my first really good laugh of the day.

'Good thing she didn't come to Mother's cocktail party,' I giggle. 'I expect she would have had Mother arrested for child exploitation as well as for possession of booze!'

'Now, now,' tuts Flossie, 'you mustn't be rude about Mrs Pilkington-Pook. It's very good of her to give you a lift each morning.'

'Well, she's certainly given me a lift this evening. I almost forgot about the Parents' Parade for a moment.'

'And you're to stop being a silly goose about that as well,' says Flossie. 'I don't know what you're imagining, but I'm sure it won't be nearly that bad.'

'We'll all be there too,' says Portia (who's beginning to look a bit pale), 'and my father will probably wear his stethoscope and listen to Ms Worhause's chest!'

'And I expect my father will wear his Hawaiian shirt and

tasteful recycled bin bag coat

I expect the cardboard shoes would go a bit soggy in the rain

BAN BOOZE
Mop up Knights!

his open-toed sandles,' Minnie adds.

'And by next week Granny and Grandpa will be even older that they are now,' says Mercedes.

'Oh, all right,' I say as poor Portia makes a mad dash for the loo. 'I'll try not to think about it till it's all over.'

Lying in bed in Heaven that night I think about all the things that have happened during the day. I suppose it all went wrong from the start when I missed seeing Adam throbbing on his motorbike. Now not only have I got the Fashion Show to plan for but there's the Valentine disco and Parents' Evening to fret about. Honestly you would think all this worry would have worn me away to a SHADOW by now, but the wobble factor this evening was well into triple figures and I still haven't made any Life Changes yet.

chapter nine

Custard Cream Crisis

IT'S BEEN ALMOST two weeks and my life is still un-changed. I haven't been able to make any proper plans for the Fashion Show or think about what to wear to the disco – I've just been sooo worried about this Parents' Evening thing. I just know it's going to go badly. Mother is never going to understand my career choice and even Ms Worhause won't be able to talk sense into her. And Potty will be *too* embarrassing as usual. What will Ms Worhause think?

We're just about to set off to the school. We're waiting for a taxi as Flossie is busy cooking supper and the rest of us can't drive. Potty appears at the top of the stairs in his cord jacket, checked shirt and old school tie (all right so far . . .) with his red and white PYJAMA TROUSERS, checked slippers and, as a finishing touch, his PANAMA HAT! For goodness' sake! It's a freezing cold, gloomy January evening.

Mother smiles absently at him as she flings her pashmina over her shoulder, smoothes down her Chanel two-piece, and adds just a touch more Super-Pout Petunia lipstick.

'Potty . . .' I say '. . . do you think the panama hat is a good idea?'

'Absolutely, Cherub. Got to keep the sun off the old brain box. Might overheat otherwise.'

It's dark outside for goodness' sake. But it's no use arguing. My only hope of salvation is that the taxi will lose its way or break down or turn into a pumpkin before we get to school. But just when you need a fairy godmother there is never one around, is there?

The taxi makes it to school in one piece, and Potty ties Stinker to the banister rail in the main hall and tells him to behave (might as well ask him not to breathe). There's nobody about as Mother, Potty and I find our way to my classroom.

Only Vivi the Scivvy's parents are waiting to see Ms Worhause when we get there. They smile at Potty in a pitying sort of way, but he's full of the joys of spring (in January). He raises his panama hat, and bowing a little says, 'Fear not, I come in peace,' before plopping himself down next to Vivi's very timid-looking mother and asking her about her opinions on rap music.

I just pray that it will be our turn soon and nobody else will come in with their parents and see us. I try to stand as far away from Potty and Mother as possible, hoping that people won't realise they are anything to do with me.

Mother has her compact out and is dusting age-defying, reflective skin enhancer on to her nose when Ms Worhause invites us in.

This is not going so badly. I'm almost beginning to think it might be all right. Ms Worhause (who is just so fab) doesn't

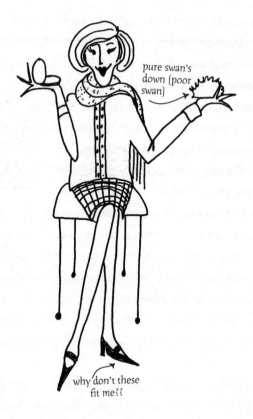

pure swan's down (poor swan)

why don't these fit me??

seem in the least bit surprised by the state of my parents. In fact, my mother and Ms Worhause spend a lot of the time discussing skincare products while Potty hums in the background. Ms Worhause also does her best to persuade Mother that cooking is a real job, but of course Mother is not convinced and still thinks that I should be a beautician (hence the skincare discussion). At least Ms Worhause is on my side, and Potty says he thinks cooking is at the 'hub of the universe', whatever that means. So, I suppose it could be much worse.

I'm just thinking about how the meeting is almost successfully over when I hear a bit of a crash from the next room and, peeking through the door at the refreshment table, I can see that good old Stinker has escaped from the hall and is standing on what used to plate of custard creams, having polished off the lot. Vivi's mother is trembling a bit and someone is laughing loudly. Creeping out of Ms Worhause's room, I see that the owner of the loud laugh is SYDNEY! No,

just before he managed to scoff the last two bix

please don't let this be happening. Not Sydney in all his slimy slitheriness. Not Sydney in the *same room* as my totally loony parents. I'll never, ever hear the end of this!

He makes his way across the room, still smiling and chuckling slightly. 'Mr and Mrs Cookson Potts, how lovely to meet you. I'm Sydney, one of Angel's close friends.'

WHAT? Has the world gone MAD? The closest he's ever been to me is *at least* arm's length, and even *that* was too close. I have to get my parents and Stinker away from here before any of them do anything else that Sydney can torture me with. I grab Potty's hand and say, 'Come on, you must both see the playing fields by moonlight, and I'm sure Stinker could do with a bit of a run after all those biscuits.'

'Starlit soccer,' says Potty. 'Sounds wonderful, Cherub. Come on, Stinks, let's go and see if we can make a striker of you.' And with that we escape from Sydney's sickening smile and scuttle down the stairs.

Mother is at least two flights of stairs behind us. I shout to her to hurry up and she calls back, 'I don't know why you're in such a hurry, dahling . . . I've so enjoyed meeting Ms Racehorse. And I'd really rather like to linger a little and perhaps look at the painting exhibition in the hall. Anyway, dahling, my heels are much too high to hurry.'

Why can't Mother wear nice flat, recycled cardboard shoes like Mrs Sophie Something-Hyphenated? Now we have to wait around for her to totter down the stairs and then risk being spotted while she does her 'I'm terribly interested in art' bit.

The coast is clear when we get to the hall, but I'm still sticky with dread after Sydney's slimings and can't help hopping up and down a bit in the hope that it might hurry everything up. Then, just as I catch Potty on all fours playing fantasy football with Stinker, the door opens and who should come in? ADAM. He stops. He looks at Mother. He looks at Potty and Stinker. He looks at me. He raises one eyebrow, shakes his head slightly and, with a whisper of a smile, he turns around and leaves.

panama hat

it's quite sweet really, but they're both totally bonkers

THAT WAS IT! The moment I've been waiting ALL MY LIFE for. The first time Adam has EVER looked at me and I'm surrounded by my freaky family AND I forgot to bend my knees . . . Could life be any more awful??

Wobble factor in the bath tonight is off the scale. I have to do something soon . . . It may even be too late to ever get Adam to notice me again. TOTAL depression.

chapter ten

Heavenly Body, Here I Come

ON SATURDAY MORNING, two days after the First (and probably the Last) Time Adam Ever Noticed Me, I'm sitting at the kitchen table as usual with Mercedes, Minnie, Portia and Flossie.

'Don't worry, Angel,' says Mercedes, 'I don't expect Adam even realised it was you.'

'And I bet he didn't laugh. He was probably just smiling at you. Sympathetically,' Portia adds.

'I don't want sympathy!' I squeak. 'I want passion and adoration or adulation or whatever it's called . . . and rides on his motorbike and lunch with his parents . . .'

'Steady on,' cautions Flossie. 'He hasn't even said hello yet, has he?'

Flossie's so good at being down to earth (and making iced chocolate brownies – Portia has already had four).

I try to think about something else. I wonder whether J Oliver Esq. has a better chocolate brownie recipe . . . (gosh, there goes my pounding heart again).

George suddenly appears with a book under his arm, doing some more study leaving. Minnie starts fluttering all over the place and, within about a minute, has already offered to make George three cups of tea, but so far he still doesn't seem to be responding to her full-on flirting.

'Anyway, Angel, it's the Valentine disco soon. You'll have to get Adam to notice properly then,' says Minnie, miraculously turning her attention away from George for a few seconds. 'What a pity you can't come to the disco, George.' She does her 'shy' smile.

It's just so weird to see Minnie flirting with George. I mean, he's like my brother and she's almost like a sister, and it feels quite spooky to have her giving out all these 'I fancy you rotten' signals. What I can't understand is why? Flossie thinks Minnie's insecure. But I can't grasp why anyone who looks like Minnie would be insecure. It's all a mystery to me . . . I really must have a serious talk to George and find out if he realises what's going on.

'You're a silly goose, Angel' says Flossie. 'The evening wasn't nearly as bad as it could have been. It sounds like Mercedes had all her problems sorted out by her grandparents and Ms Worhause,' (they had worked out exactly what exams she should take to do her sporty whatsits), 'Portia's parents didn't complain about the germs, and your mother and Potty enjoyed themselves. Maybe this Adam isn't as wonderful as you think he is.'

'Oh, but he is, Flossie!' I practically shout, ignoring all her other comments. 'You don't understand, you've never *seen* Adam. He is *sooo* sexy . . . I just have to find a way to be his Eve.'

Portia makes a very rude joke about fig leaves and George says he thinks Adam sounds like a total poser, riding his motorbike to school and strutting about in his leathers. Although what it's got to do with him, I'm sure I don't know.

'I bet if I was about two stone lighter he would realise that I'm the girl of his dreams.'

Minnie does a quick calculation. 'That would mean you would have to lose two pounds a day for the next – '

'Don't be daft,' Portia interrupts. 'You're gorgeous as you are and what would we all do if you stopped making scrummy food for us?'

'You're such a friend, Portia,' I say, 'trying to make me feel better. But I'm sure that if there was less of me Adam would be more likely to notice me.'

'If there was less of you, he would be *less* likely to see you,' George grumbles. (Why is George always so grumpy? Or perhaps he's being cool – it can be difficult to tell with George.)

'Oh George, you do say such clever things,' says Minnie.

Mercedes shoots me a look of concern. 'You wouldn't be *you* if you got all skinny, and I'd worry about you if you didn't eat enough.' She's so sweet. She worries about everyone, all the time. It's amazing that she's got enough concern to go around.

'Well, I'm not that thrilled to be *me* at the moment,' I say. 'I'd quite like to be the little slim person that's inside me instead.'

'All these girls stopping eating and going anorexic and making themselves sick . . .' says Flossie, shaking her head. 'It's a crying shame. I like nothing better than to see people sitting down to a good meal and really enjoying it. If this boy wants you to be something you're not, he's not for you.'

'I quite agree,' says Portia, helping herself to another brownie. 'Food can't do you any harm, as long as it is hygienically prepared.' Where does she put all the grub she tucks away? It's a complete mystery.

'Well,' I say, getting up, 'I'm sorry, but I have made my

decision. I've been thinking about making Life Changes ever since the start of the Christmas holidays and I've decided that there's only one thing for it. I shall go on a DIET.'

Flossie goes off into her bedroom tutting loudly and Mercedes is making her prune face again. Meanwhile, I nip upstairs and return with a pile of *Teen Speak* magazines.

'Right. Find me a diet,' I say and hand the magazine round.

'No thanks,' says George, and he wanders off to go and be grumpy upstairs.

After we've done our extensive research, I decide to plump (!) for the Cabbage Diet. This, at last, will be the start of my Life Changes. I must say I don't much like the sound of it, except that it says it works very quickly and I only have a short time to go until the disco. Also, you can eat as much cabbage as you like, and any diet that says you can eat as much of something as you like can't be all bad, can it?

We start discussing how many cabbages I'm likely to eat in a day, and Minnie tries to work out how many calories per mouthful of cabbage.

'You'll have to wash it really well, unless you want to be digesting germs,' says Portia. 'And what about protein? It really isn't a very balanced diet, Angel. Our bodies need all sorts of different vitamins and nutrients to function properly.'

'It'll be fine,' I assure her. 'I'll be like a caterpillar chomping my way through oceans of green stuff before I turn into a beautiful butterfly.' In my cabbage fantasy I imagine myself in three weeks' time. The Size 16 Angel will have magically transformed into a perfect Size 12 Angel. All my wobbles and worries will melt away together. My skin will gleam. My hair will be glossy. My eyes will be bright with the prospect of LURVE . . .

'Just as long as you don't turn into one of those creepy moths,' says Mercedes, who is still looking concerned.

'Don't worry, Mercedes. I shall only do it for as long as it takes Adam to realise that I'm his Eve, and then we'll ride off into the sunset on his motorbike and celebrate our new-found love with homemade chocolate eclairs and ice cream.'

'Shouldn't that be apples?' says Mercedes (GROAN).

Minnie gives up calculating and says, 'Portia was right, Angel – you *are* lovely just the way you are. And confident. I wish I was as confident as you.'

'Total poo,' I say. 'You know I'm a big wobbly thing. You ask Mother – she's forever telling me that I "gallumph". She'll be thrilled when she finds that a huge wodge of me has disappeared.'

'Well, I think it's a shame . . .' says Minnie, and then they all start on about my personality being generous like my body (is that supposed to be comforting?). Anyway, what would *they* know? They've never been anything but tiny.

The girlies do their best to put me off the idea, but I'm actually feeling really excited about the diet. I know it's going to be the answer to all my problems – well, most of them anyway. I know Adam will leave that gang of boys with bikes and skinny blonde bimbos behind. I'll be just so much more fascinating than his head gasket or whatever it is he's always taking apart in the bike shed. He'll choose to spend every moment with me and I'll cook him divine dinners, and he'll never wave to other girls again . . .

But first I have to convince Flossie that the diet *is* a wonderful idea and get her to help me organise it all.

Flossie is very scratchy about the whole thing and says, 'Heavens to Betsy! Whoever heard of such a thing? Eating cabbage for breakfast? It's not natural. Cabbage should only be served as part of a meal and have plenty of butter on it.'

I explain that there should be no butter at all, but that I am allowed a little salt and pepper, and that I can have my cabbage as soup, steamed, raw or, for special occasions, stir-fried in a drop of olive oil.

Flossie grumbles a lot more. 'It could do a body no end of damage only eating one thing like that. Even a rabbit has a dandelion every now and then. I don't know, Angel. I really do think it sounds most unhealthy. A girl needs some padding in weather like this . . . you'll catch your death of cold with no fat on your bones.'

Flossie goes on a bit more, but seeing my desperation, she finally does agree to buy the cabbages. She asks me what type I'd like to start with. I had no idea there were so many different sorts of cabbage, but I think that 'Savoy' sounds quite exotic, so I suggest we start with some of them.

Just then I look up to find Potty standing in the doorway in his wig and gown (having just hung the washing out for Flossie).

'What's all this, little Cherub?' he asks, looking at the table strewn with magazines. I try to explain.

'Dye it?' he asks. 'Why do you want to dye it? It's a spiffing colour as it is.'

I try again. 'I'm not going to dye anything, Potty. I'm going on a *diet* to get slim and gorgeous.'

'Cherub! Don't do it! Beastly business, dieting. Tried it myself once. Got so hungry I could quite happily have eaten Stinker here.'

'Yuck,' I say, 'but this is going to be a really well-organised diet, Potty, and you won't recognise me when I'm boot-lace thin.'

Potty looks really unhappy. 'I love my little Cherub just as she is.' He looks wistful for a while and then says, 'I think I feel a pamphlet coming on. Yes, I definitely feel a pamphlet coming on. I shall call it "Flab is Fab" and I shall give it to all the jolly people coming out of the Harrods Food Hall.'

He potters off, and with a mournful glance back at me, starts humming, 'I love you just the way you are . . .' He can be such a sweetie sometimes, but I am not to be deterred. This is the beginning of my Life Changes.

ahh! – this is Potty all wrinkly with worry

green and white p'jams – his favourites

81

I will have to pretend to have a terrible cold tomorrow so that I can skip Sunday lunch with the family. I don't really want Mother to know about the diet. For one thing, I know she wouldn't be interested anyway, and for another I want to surprise her with the completely new, slim me that's going to go to the Valentine disco.

SO . . . You can imagine my surprise when Mother finds her way up to Heaven later that day (after I've had my first, deeply unsatisfying raw cabbage meal) and says she wants to have a 'woman to woman' talk with me. Usually we have ex-model to dough-ball chats, so this is something COMPLETELY new.

'Angel,' she begins, 'I'm very concerned to hear that you're going on some ridiculous diet.'

I'm stunned enough by the fact that she has teetered up to Heaven in her Jimmy Choo daytime diamante mules . . . but expressing CONCERN about me? All I can do is open my mouth and gawp at her.

'You absolutely do not need to go on some stupid crash diet . . .'

I have to stop her there. '*What* are you talking about? I thought you wanted me to be slim! You're always telling me I've eaten enough . . . you squawk at me for "gallumphing" and . . . and you make me feel like I'm taking up too much space or denting the cushions or looking huge and untidy wherever I go . . .'

'Angel, please . . . I'm only thinking of what's best for – '

'*Who?* For me? You've never shown any interest in me – only what I look like . . .'

82

And then I can't stop myself. It must be the lack of proper food making me light-headed. I feel a sort of mini-explosion inside. Here I am finally making a real Life Change and Mother wants to stop me. She's part of the reason I'm *doing* this. Before I know it things are out of my mouth that I didn't know were there.

'You don't know anything *about* me! You don't care what GCSEs I take, just as long as I don't eat too much. I . . . I'm amazed you even know where my bedroom is. How can you say you're *concerned*? The only thing you're ever *concerned* about is the latest beauty treatment. You don't care about ME at all and now you tell me you're concerned that I'm not

my halo!

heavenly bed

having a mumsy-
and-daughter
moment

Prada,
dahling

eating enough? Look at you! You don't eat anything and you're TINY . . .'

I'm all pink and shaking now. Mother sits down on the bed next to me and pats my hand. I can hardly believe it, but there seem to be tears in her eyes.

'You're quite wrong, Angel. I *do* care very much about you . . . I admit that I have been very stupid about food all my life. But now my bones are becoming brittle, my skin has lost all the lovely softness that your skin has and I have to have endless treatments to stop my hair falling out. I was a fool to think that being thin was important. Angel dahling, you don't need to be skinny. Look at Sophie Dahl – she's beautiful.'

'Yes . . .' I say a bit shakily, 'but she's loosing weight now.'

'I know.' And all my friends in the fashion business say she's losing her looks as well. Some people simply *should* be bigger. I know I say things to you about potatoes and gallumphing, but most of the time I'm not even *thinking* what I'm saying – it's just a habit I've got into. Sometimes I even imagine it's funny – just a tease. Dahling, please don't do this cranky diet.'

With that she pats my hand again and dabbing her eyes with her tiny lace hanky, she gets up and teeters downstairs.

I'm so stunned by all the things that Mother said, and it leaves me feeling weird inside. I honestly didn't think she would care the tiniest bit about the diet. And telling me all that stuff about herself – she's never ever done that before. In fact, I don't think we've ever really talked about *anything* before . . . Perhaps she does notice me and worry about me. But if she doesn't want me to get thin, then why *does* she tut when I eat too many potatoes? It can't just be habit . . .

I can't work it out. I need something to take my mind off it. A chocolate biscuit . . . a warm pancake with syrup . . . NO, I'm *not* going to eat. I shall sit in the bath with a face pack on and read J.O.N.C. instead.

As I lie in bed later that night, it occurs to me that this is the first time I haven't eaten food to comfort myself. I can barely believe it. I've been thinking all night about what everybody has said. A lot of it was really kind and lovely but I just HAVE to find out if being slim will change my life . . . and the only way to do that is to carry on. So I have decided that now that I've made such a good start with the diet, I shall have to go on regardless.

chapter eleven

THE DIET

Sunday

8.30 a.m. Get up. Sneeze a lot (pretend - to make sure I can get out of having Sunday lunch).

8.40 a.m. Leap downstairs in sporty, exercising sort of way.

8.45 a.m. Breakfast. Cabbage (raw - YUCK).

10.30 a.m. Leap back upstairs.

10.35 a.m. Do stretches (not sure what these are - usually it's my clothes not me that are doing the stretching).

11.05 a.m. Break wind.

11.20 a.m. Ditto.

11.40 a.m. Ditto.

11.50 a.m. Do press-up.

12.10 p.m. Early lunch in bedroom (boiled cabbage with salt and pepper – oh GOODY). Mother doesn't come up to see if I'm OK.

12.32 p.m. Sneeze a lot more (passing Mother's room).

12.15 p.m. Break wind.

1.00 p.m. Ditto.

2.30 p.m. Ditto.

2.35 p.m. Try doing aerobic 'steps' workout on the stairs.

2.36 p.m. Read mags and watch telly and think about food for the Fashion Show.

2.38 p.m. Stop thinking about food.

3.04 p.m. Break wind.

4.00 p.m. Cup of tea (no milk).

6.00 p.m. Steamed cabbage.

8.00 p.m. Wobble factor unchanged.

8.30 p.m. So bored, decide to go to bed. Spend very blustery and faint-makingly smelly night in Heaven.

Monday

7.20 a.m. Wake up. Do press-ups (well, press-up, actually).

8.00 a.m. Eat cabbage.

8.20 a.m. Make Mrs Sophie Something-Hyphenated's car even smellier.

8.45 a.m. School.

11.15 a.m. Break. Break wind.

12.30 p.m. Packed lunch (soggy cold cabbage).

End of each lesson: rush to loo to explode in private.

4.30 p.m. Get home. Small cabbage snack.

4.40 p.m. Wind-propelled up to Heaven.

5.00–7.00 p.m. Homework blown about bedroom by cabbage windy whiffs.

7.30 p.m. Raw cabbage dinner with lemon juice (yum – NOT).

10.00 p.m. Bath with homemade jacuzzi effect. Wobble factor unchanged.

10.30 p.m. Bed. Dream of hurricanes and cream buns.

Tuesday

Ditto.

Wednesday

Ditto, but Flossie tries to tempt me with vegetable crisps. I DO
NOT SUCCUMB.

Thursday

Ditto, until 5.00 p.m. when I finally decide I CAN'T GO ON LIKE
THIS. All I've lost is my sense of humour, and how can I go to
the disco if I'm going to be wind-powered around the dance
floor, gassing everyone out in the process?

No, that's it. I give up. I admit defeat (and de fat). Here
Endeth My First and Last Diet.

Something Nicer Than Cabbage
(Vegetable Crisps)

vegetable oil for frying   *2 sweet potatoes*
sea salt   *2 uncooked beetroot*
2 parsnips   *2 carrots*

You need a deep-fryer for these really – it's much easier (and much less dangerous) than doing them in the frying pan. In fact, please don't try these in a frying pan – they spit and splutter and hot oil goes EVERYWHERE.

Heat the oil in the deep-fryer to 160°C. Peel and slice the veggies as thinly as possible (try to keep the slices even). Then put them on a tray and deep-fry in little batches until they are golden brown and crisp. Drain and put them on kitchen paper and sprinkle with sea salt. Yummy, and obviously SO good for you because they are veggies, right?

chapter twelve

Dress to Impress and Cake Up the Make-up

THE CABBAGE DIET officially ended on Thursday the 23rd of January. So for the next couple of weeks we do all the deeply dull school-type things as usual. It rains a lot and when it's not raining it's freezing, so Flossie and I have to make a lot of VERY delicious little yummies to keep everyone's spirits up. It's even nicer to be cooking again after the cabbage fiasco and I spend my time thinking up recipes while I'm standing around on school playing fields. They MAKE us do sports even when the temperature is sub-zero. I have to admit that Flossie is right about a girl needing extra padding in the winter. It's so cold on the hockey pitch that even I (encased in thermals, tights, thick socks, tracky bums, games shirt, three jerseys and tracksuit hoody) think that I might be getting chilblains in places that chilblains definitely shouldn't be. I suppose if I ran about a bit I *might* get warmer, but for someone who doesn't run, even the idea of it is exhausting.

Sydney is as sickening as ever – he's so slimy, he really should freeze to the pavement in this weather, but nothing stops him oozing around. And as for Adam, he's always so muffled up . . . in his leathers it's hard to know *what* he's noticing.

Still, there's always the disco to think about and the Fashion Show to plan. It's freezing cold inside as well, so the four of us practise our dance moves along the school corridors to keep warm while we fantasise about the amazing things we'll wear to the disco. Diet or no diet, I WILL get Adam to notice me.

Minnie has promised to bring some of the wondrous things she's made to my house and Portia and Mercedes are going to bring ALL their clothes so we can have a proper 'dress to impress' session in preparation for the disco.

FINALLY, Friday the 14th of February has arrived, and we lay all our clothing options out on my heavenly bed.

It's 1.32 p.m. We have just six short hours and twenty-eight minutes to GET READY. I've been practising my disco moves this morning. Thank goodness the windy whiffs and savoy smellies have gone the same way as the cabbages – out of my life. I'm ready to party.

The girlies have brought bagfuls of possible drop-dead gorgeous. We've got the shoes, belts, earrings, glittery bits and fishnet tights one end of the bed and at the other end there are posh tops, trashy tops, slinky tops and sparkly tops. Next to those we have tiny skirts, much bigger skirts (mine, natch), long skirts, skin-tight jeans, baggy jeans, jeans with sparkly seams. Then there are smart trousers, semi-smart trousers and trousers it would be smarter not to wear. It looks like a fabulous, in-your-dreams jumble sale and I haven't even mentioned the cosmetics yet!

'Why don't you try this, Angel?' says Mercedes holding out a bright red lace-up corset.

'You so have to be joking,' I say, looking at the tiny strip of red stuff that she's holding.

'Go on, try it. Look – it's all stretchy. It would fit anyone.'

While I scuttle into the bathroom to squish myself into this little riot of red, Mercedes is seeing what frilly panties look like over her jeans. Surprisingly, it looks rather good but would she dare wear them like that?

'Someone will have to lace me up,' I trill from the bathroom. Minnie struggles a bit with the laces and I emerge, pink and panting, in what can only be described as a body condom. It's SO tight that the barrage balloons have popped up into my armpits and I can't lower my arms. I have to admit that I do now have an awesome waist, but that's only because what used to be around my waist has now appeared below the bottom of the corset, giving a sort of rubber ring effect just above my hips.

'Do you know . . .' I pant, 'I don't thing this does a lot for me!'

'No,' they all reply. Mercedes concedes, 'Perhaps it's not *entirely* you.'

'*This*, however, is en-TYRE-ly me,' I say as I prod the offending spare tyre.

Minnie giggles. 'Perhaps you could get a puncture and ask Adam to mend it for you.'

'He'd have to get his spanner out, then!' splutters Portia.

'Enough!' I snort. 'I can't laugh in this. Let me get into something I can breathe in before I think about Adam and his spanner.'

Portia is laughing so hysterically that she puts her head through the arm hole of Minnie's sixties-style, tie-dyed vest top. This makes us all giggling wrecks, and she squeaks, 'What's happened to my other arm? Help me someone! I can't move, I'm totally armless . . .'

It's no good, we need a break and good old Flossie has been making pancakes. So we hurry off to the basement for a quick pick-me-up before we go back to the 'swap and search' for the perfect party outfit.

The pancakes are warm and golden, just crispy around the edges and Flossie has put out a bowl full of whipped cream, a bottle of maple syrup and a jug of my thick hot chocolate sauce to put on them. A girl needs extra energy at a time like this.

We discuss the pros and cons of glitter in the hair – fab and groovy or expensive dandruff? – around the table while we scoff down the pancakes. Then we pound back up the stairs and begin the serious preparations.

Among the things that Minnie brought are all sorts of ter-rific things that she's made. Fringy skirts, little painted beanie hats (which look superb on her, but which make me look as if I'm wearing an egg cosy), decorated T-shirts . . . She has also brought her 'customising kit' with her, so when I finally decide to wear a black, sleeveless T-shirt (so flattering, black) she offers to customise it for me.

In the twinkling of an eye, she has decorated the neck of the shirt and written 'DISCO DIVA' in diamante studs across the front. Of course she doesn't think that she's done it very well, but it looks totally professional and wildly expensive. I wouldn't normally want *anything* to draw attention to the Danger Zone, but when I try it on I have to admit that the sparkle sort of camouflages the out-of-control wobbly bits.

Minnie is rattling on excitedly about me modelling one of her tops for the Fashion Show. Luckily Portia suddenly puts a stop to this bonkers idea when she jumps up and dives into the bathroom and comes back with two loo rolls. This makes the rest of us ask, 'What are you going to do with that?'

does she really think she'll get the whole roll in there?

'Watch,' she says, and she proceeds to stuff yards and yards of loo paper into her bra.

'Oh, brilliant!' Mercedes exclaims, and she starts to do the same. Portia suddenly has Page-Three boobs while I'm left wishing that I had some loo paper I could take OUT of my bra.

'You see? You're SO lucky, Angel. You'll never have to do this,' says Minnie as her T-shirt gets tighter and tighter.

'At least you can choose whether it's going to be a loo paper day or not,' I retort. 'There's always a family pack of Andrex in my bra, whether I want it there or not!'

'Oh, don't moan,' says Mercedes. 'At least you haven't got

half a tonne of metal in your mouth, and you look great in that T-shirt.'

I must say that I am feeling really rather pleased with this T-shirt. I thrash about through all the possible 'bottom halves' spread across my bed, to find the perfect partner for my delicious new top.

Of course, I must bear in mind that I will probably be riding on the back of a motorbike (the red, throbbing one) by the end of the evening . . . Finally I decide on my most favourite, totally cool, figure-hugging vintage jeans. Mercedes lends me a wide, studded belt (that must be miles too big for her) which has a sort of biker feel to it, and I really think I'm getting there.

Minnie is looking MUCH too pretty in a little floaty skirt that she has designed and made, of course, and a wicked T-shirt with a huge pink rose hand-painted on the front. One of her homemade crochet beanie hats completes her bo-ho, beatnik, post-flower power look. We have to reassure her that none of it actually looks homemade. And it's true – she really looks as if she's stepped straight out of *Vogue*.

Portia, meanwhile, has gone for full-on funky punky (mind you, she's a very well-scrubbed punk). She's wearing a ripped and pinned snowy white vest top, black studded jeans, high-heeled boots and a red studded collar around her neck.

Mercedes is wearing a short black skirt with a black corset top very like the red one I tried on (although the effect is a bit different on her) and black strappy sandles. She has a 'dia-mond' choker, which she thinks will sparkle more than her brace and direct attention away from her mouth. She looks like someone out of a CK Two advert.

I opt for my divine L.K. Bennett kitten-heel mules, which finish any outfit off to perfection.

Once we've made sure our hair is root-to-tip superb, I creep downstairs to borrow just a smudge of Mother's Smouldering Smooch lipstick and find Stinker standing, triumphantly in the middle of her dressing table with half a Chanel lipstick hanging out of his mouth (and it's not even his colour). The remains of several others are scattered around his paws. I decide to pretend I didn't catch him red-handed (or should that be red-mouthed?) and tiptoe back upstairs again.

I'm feeling pretty jolly super and my friends are looking DIVINE. Six hours of full-on, non-stop, DESPERATELY hard work has done the business. We are ready!

We run into Mother and Potty on our way downstairs. They

he's got very good taste in lipstick!

are going to the opera together. They go out a lot – mostly to parties – but I don't think they ever speak to each other when they are there. Potty is either the 'life and soul' or asleep, and Mother does her best to ignore him whichever he's doing. They both love the opera, though (v. dull, *I* think) and Potty loves to sing along (usually a different song). 'Adds a bit of excitement, Cherub.' . . . Yes, especially when he gets up at the end and takes a bow wearing his pyjamas and spotted bow tie!

As we pass them, Mother tells me to 'stand up straight'. She's always got to make some pooey comment. And with all that stuff about how concerned she was about me . . . Nothing's changed around here. It was obviously all a load of twoddle. Couldn't she just this once admit that I'm looking fab? And besides, I *can't* stand up straight – she just doesn't realise how important it is for Eve to be smaller than Adam.

Potty tells us that we remind him of a day he spent on Brighton Beach. We think that's a compliment, but it's difficult to be certain.

When we get down to the kitchen for a quick snack before leaving, Flossie says we 'all look a sight for sore eyes' which is another one of those sayings that you're never quite sure about. And George, who seems to have stopped studying and started standing around in the kitchen, glances quickly at us, then trudges back upstairs. Minnie is FURIOUS that after all the hard work he doesn't even notice her. Boys.

My Own Amazing Energy-Giving Chocolate Sauce

at least half a Mars bar per person
a little double cream (or a lot, if you're feeling naughty)

a sprinkling of chocolate chips

This is SOOO easy-peasy. Cut the Mars bar into small pieces. Put the cut-up bars into a bowl that fits tightly over a pan of not-quite-boiling water (or put the pieces into a double boiler, if you have one), until it melts. When all the lumpy bits have disappeared, stir in some double cream and if you like little surprise bits of chocolate in your sauce, sprinkle in some chocolate chips. GOLLY!

chapter thirteen

Rock 'n' Roll or Sausage Roll?

THE DISCO'S WILD. When we arrive – fashionably late, because Flossie only drives at about three miles per hour – the place is thrumming. There's a DJ (he's quite a cutie actually) and he's playing groovesome dance music, so loud it makes your tummy wobble (well, it makes *my* tummy wobble). The decorations are brilliant. You could hardly recognise the boring old school hall. There are two disco balls, and the doors and windows are covered with black paper with huge red cut-out hearts all over them. There are swags of red crepe across the ceiling and masses of heart-shaped balloons hanging in bunches in the corners. Someone has made a great big cut-out Cupid with bow and arrows, which is attached to the wall bars and surrounded by glittery hearts.

Mr Cutie DJ also has a smoke machine, and through the mist we can see that everyone must have spent at *least* all day getting ready. Even the saddest saddos look almost groovy.

We move on to the dance floor and start to sort of wiggle about a bit, all the time looking to see who's where and what they're doing. Yes, all right, I admit that really I am only look-ing for Adorable Adam. Where can he be? . . . I suddenly think I can hear the roar of his throbbing motorbike above the music, when Mercedes shouts, 'Look at Scarlet!'

I look to where she is pointing and there is 'I think I'm a superstar' Scarlet, prancing about in a floor-length strapless red dress. And she's got a huge feather boa, which she's wrap-ping around some poor unsuspecting Upper Sixth boy, trying to drag him on to the dance floor. She's doing a kind of fla-menco thing, with lots of heel-clacking and tossing about of her hair. Her little slave, Vivi, is watching, spellbound, as Scarlet starts to sing along to the music. She sounds like badly

a truly
frightened
boy

ear lobe
stretchers

who does she
think she is,
Julia Roberts?

oiled brakes, but you can see she thinks she's WONDERFUL. To top it all, she's wearing her sunglasses – oh, *pleeease*. I expect she's worried she'll be recognised and mobbed by her adoring fans!

Mercedes drifts away with Paul, who is really nice, but just a teensy bit spotty. He's in our year, but in another class, so we don't see him often. She looks quite happy and is doing her own version of Scarlet's Spanish thing, but with more impressive hair tossing.

I turn to speak to Minnie and find she is surrounded by bimbo boys with their tongues hanging out. But we all knew that would happen. She doesn't look very pleased to see any of them and I suspect that she is still pining away for goofy George.

That just leaves Portia and me doing our *Top of the Pops* dance routine. Just as I'm really getting into the hip-grinding and shoulder-shimmying, I happen to look up and see . . . HIM – gasp. Adam. He's standing across the dance floor talking to some weirdo from his year and looking fridge cool, with black jeans and a figure-hugging T-shirt. Just for a fleeting moment I think I catch a glimpse of a heel on his boot, but obviously that's a trick of the light.

Has he seen me yet? Maybe he has already spotted me and is plucking up the courage to come and whisk me away. I don't know what to do . . . I mustn't gawp. Just try to keep dancing as if you don't care, Angel, I tell myself.

I'm doing my best to follow my own advice when HE looks up . . . He's seen me!!! He's coming over . . . My stomach has every butterfly in the British Isles inside it. My knees turn to jelly (which is just as well because I would have forgotten to bend them otherwise). My mouth goes dry. This is IT. Try to swallow. Try to look cool. Here he comes . . . and he . . .

ASKS PORTIA TO DANCE!!! Does he even look at me? NO, HE DOES NOT. And is Portia going to dance with him? YES, SHE IS. What is she doing? Has she had her conscience surgically removed??? He's supposed to be MINE!!

She looks back at me over her shoulder and gives me a sort of worried look, but then she looks back at Adam and doesn't look worried at all. I want to scream at her, 'You're meant to be my friend!' But what's the use? She wouldn't hear me anyway. Now they're doing this amazing dance together and she's looking slim and perfect and what am I doing? Standing there like a heffalump with my mouth wide open and no one to dance with . . .

Flossie's voice floats into my head through the drum and bass: 'Pull yourself together, Angel, and *stop gawping*.' All right. If that's how it's going to be, I'll just go and find another love god who will want me for his goddess . . .

Who am I kidding? There's only one love god and he's DANCING WITH PORTIA.

I can't be seen by everyone, standing there like a jelly, so I glide as gracefully as I can off the dance floor and go and stand near the disco. Perhaps Mr Cutie DJ will ask me to dance. That would show Adam. I mean, I don't have to content myself with wasting my time with a schoolboy. Oh no, not me. I'm looking for a REAL MAN. I give Mr Cutie DJ one of my most winning smiles and . . . Already he's responding to my magnetic charms. He's stepping off the podium to ask me to dance . . .

Uh-oh, think fast Angel – Mr Cutie DJ has SHRUNK. He is about level with my Disco Divas (to put it delicately). He's grinning like the Cheshire Cat and I look around just in time to catch SYDNEY laughing at me. Is this a grotty party, or is this a grotty party?

With my usual lightning quick wit, I ask Mr No Longer Cutie DJ to play an old Madonna song, then he says 'OK' and climbs back on to his podium. I turn around and give Sydney a 'There, you see? I just wanted to make a request' look. He's still laughing, but at least I feel a bit less of a twit. Now what am I going to do?

I spend some time pretending to be really fascinated by the dancing, tapping my foot and clapping my hands a bit. But looking at the dancing is actually the LAST thing I want to do, because just over there, out of the corner of my eye, I can see one of my BEST FRIENDS with HIM. And in front of me there's Scarlet in her feather boa and sunglasses, doing goodness knows what to some poor little Year Nine boy. UGH! It's all completely sick-making.

'You're looking a bit lonely, Jelly Potts . . .'

104

Yes, of course, just to make my misery complete, there he is – Slimy Sydney in all his Slitheriness.

'I'm not in the least bit lonely,' I tell him, BBC voice in full swing. 'I just love watching people dance. It's SO amusing!'

'I bet you could make some awesome moves,' he says, studying 'DISCO DIVA' much too closely for comfort.

'The only moves I'm going to make are away from you,' I declare, turning away from him dramatically and hitting my nose on one of the speakers. Then I can hear him laughing again . . . Why don't I just shoot myself now? Can this get any more GROTESQUE??

Where are my lovely friends when I need them? I just catch sight of Minnie surrounded by boys and I suppose Mercedes is still with Paul, although I can't see her. And as for Portia . . . I can see her through the bopping bodies, *still* dancing with HIM.

Then Sydney says, 'Come on, Jelly. Come and jiggle about a bit with me. We could have some fun.' FUN?? It would be more fun swimming with piranhas.

'I'm *frightfully* sorry,' I say, with more plums in my mouth than is comfortable, 'I have another engagement!' Another engagement? What am I talking about? What sort of engagement could I possibly have at a school disco? It's not as if I've got a hundred names on my dance card and now I can't think of a single thing to be engaged with (or should that be *to*?). I give Sydney one of my best frost-filled looks, turn on my L.K. Bennett kitten heel and flounce off in the direction of the buffet table. There I become extremely 'engaged' with the food, most of which looks pretty dire, until I realise that Sydney may be following me. I quickly 'engage' myself by picking up a plate of sausage rolls and move off, full steam ahead, to the girls loos.

At least I'll be safe from Sydney in there, but what am I going to *do* all evening?

Luckily, I have to walk through the Food Tech department and I spot a battered copy of *The Return of the Naked Chef*. I grab it, knowing that Jamie would never let me down (be still, my broken heart). So, with Jamie under my arm and a plate of sausage rolls in my hand, I settle myself down for an evening of loneliness and misery in the girls loo.

But things could be a lot worse. The sausage rolls turn out to be quite scrummy, and Jamie is, as usual, totally scrummy. Girls keep popping in and out and giving me the latest news on the action on the dance floor. With a bit of luck, Sydney will think I'm up to no good in the bushes with someone much bigger than he is. And as soon as Adam realises it was me he meant to dance with, he'll find that I've vanished which will make me SO mysterious and interesting.

In fact, I'm getting on beautifully with that particular daydream when I'm rudely awakened by Scarlet the Harlot, who breezes in and tells me at great length about ALL the boys who are just desperate to dance with her. How beautiful they all think she is. How they all want to kiss her, but she couldn't let them, could she? Or they might try and sell their stories to the *News of the World* when she's FRIGHTFULLY famous. And I have to sit and listen to all this fluff and nonsense because I can't get out.

I'm just beginning to think that she must have a plug somewhere that I could pull out when she casually mentions that she saw Adam KISSING PORTIA!

'EEEEEK!' I squeal, then seeing Scarlet's look of surprise, I say, 'A spider! There's an enormous spider behind you and I think it's going to go under the hem of your dress any second now!' Well, that got her moving. She was out of there quicker than you could say 'knickers' leaving me in shreds at the thought of Portia and Adam kissing.

I'm so shredded that I think I might cry. Why should I care about my mascara now? This evening has been a total waste of make-up. My bottom lip starts trembling a bit and my nose starts getting that pre-sob pinkness . . .

Suddenly the door is flung open and in rushes Portia. I'm pretty close to knocking her over and sitting on her until all the breath has left her body, but then she splutters, 'THERE you are! I've been looking for you EVERYWHERE! Angel, I'm so sorry, but Adam is an absolute and total CREEP. He's disgusting. He could bore for Britain . . . He's SO pleased with himself and SO smarmy. He just wouldn't let me get away . . . He thinks he's God's gift . . . He's VILE and his breath smells and he tried to kiss me – tongues and everything. It was the most revolting, germ-infested experience EVER. Honestly, Angel, you are SO well out of that!' And with that it's Portia, not me, who bursts into tears.

I forgive her instantly. She is one of my best, best friends and it's obvious that she has just had a horrible time.

But as I give her a big hug and the last of the sausage rolls, I can't help wishing that it had been me, not Portia who had to fight Adam off . . .

* * *

I'm up in Heaven, tucked in under my light-as-a-cloud pink duvet, safe from all the cares of the world and BEASTLY boys. My vintage jeans and Disco Diva top are in a heap on the floor and the kitten heels are safe in their tissue-lined box.

I have to face the fact that I'm never going to be Adam's Eve and ride off to the Garden of Eden on the back of his (throbbing) red motorbike (sob). I also have to face the fact that Sydney will probably find out about my night of passion (*not*) in the girls loo with Jamie Oliver and the sausage rolls and that he will bug me about it until I'm buggier than a 'flu epidemic.

If only I could think of something that would make me feel strong and powerful, totally cool and able to cope with anything His Royal Slitheriness decides to chuck at me . . . I'm sure if I could just get along better with my body (wobble factor GIGANTIC), I would be able to deal with him. I've just got to face it: I'm not a puppy any more. This fat is not about to go anywhere. Even five days of crinkly cabbage didn't do a *thing* for me, or it. It's time to rethink my Life Changes.

Eat Your Heart Out
Heart-Shaped Biscuits

heart-shaped biscuit cutter	*100g plain flour, sifted*
85g soft unsalted butter	*1 tsp baking powder*
100g caster sugar	*150g icing sugar*
1 large egg	*pink food colouring*
½ tsp vanilla extract	

Heat oven to 180°C. Cream the butter and sugar together until really fluffy and pale. Beat in the eggs and the vanilla. Mix the baking powder into the flour, and stir the dry mixture in to the wet mixture. It might seem a bit sticky; if it does, put a little more flour in. Gather up the dough, wrap it in cling film and put it in the fridge for an hour or more.

Dust your work surface with flour and roll out the unwrapped dough to about a 0.5cm thickness. Then cut out as many hearts as you can before gathering the remaining dough up, rolling it out again and cutting a few more. Do this until all the dough is used.

Place the hearts at least 2cm apart from each other on a baking sheet and bake for 8 to 12 minutes. (They should smell wonderful.)

Once they are cooked, put the hearts on wire racks to cool.

To make the icing, add a tiny amount of water and one drop of pink food colouring to the icing sugar. Then spread the pink icing carefully over the cooled biscuits.

Share them with someone you love.

chapter fourteen

Gym and Tonics

I WAKE UP on Saturday morning feeling surprisingly bright-eyed and bushy-tailed. I decide to phone Portia and see how she is.

She still sounds very upset and she says she's had horrible dreams about aliens with germ-filled suckers instead of mouths. I try to distract her by telling her that I have to make bigger and better Life Changes since the Blow Your Mind Cabbage Diet didn't work and I still feel like a complete heffer. I explain that I need to feel strong and powerful and in control to be able to deal with all the Fashion Show organisation and to get the better of Sydney. She asks me if I've ever thought of going to the gym. I've never been to the gym – the kitchen is so much cosier. But Portia convinces me that yoga could really make me feel better without having to get all hot and glowing (so unladylike).

Just thinking about the gym makes me feel sort of sporty, so I spring down the stairs to see Flossie and decide to have a fitness breakfast (only one homemade muffin and just a smudge of jam) before phoning the others.

'Hello, my lovely friend Mercedes.'

'Goodness, Angel, what's happened to you? I thought you would be feeling all blue and miz today after Adorable Adam turned out to be Freak From Hell.'

'We must move on,' I tell her in my most grown-up, woman-of-the-world voice. 'I'm making more Life Changes.'

'What sort of changes?'

'I'm off to the gym.'

There's a stunned silence from the other end of the phone, but then, instead of giggling, Mercedes says, 'Shall I come with you?'

'Golly, Mercedes! I so hoped you'd say that. I can't exactly remember where the gym is.'

'I'll be round in a twinkling,' she chirps and puts the phone down.

Apparently we can WALK to the gym from my house. I never realised it was so close. The sun is almost shining and I'm feeling sparkly and bright. I haven't even begun the next step in my Life Changes, but I feel better already – it's amazing. On the way we meet Portia and Minnie, who have agreed to join us, and we discuss last night's action at the Valentine disco.

'Cupid certainly didn't aim his arrows very well at any of us last night,' says Minnie. (I know she's still thinking about George . . . I MUST talk to him soon.)

'I wish Cupid had shot his arrow straight into Adam's bottom,' says Portia.

Mercedes laughs. 'But that would have made him fall in love with someone.'

111

'He's *already* in love with someone – HIMSELF,' sniffles Portia.

'None of us ended up with a valentine, did we?' I say, glancing at Mercedes. 'Or *did* we?'

She goes a little bit pink (well, she doesn't actually go *pink* because she's that lovely coffee colour, but she flushes nonetheless). 'Paul's very nice,' she responds very slowly.

'And did he say he couldn't kiss you because of your brace?' I ask.

'No, but . . .'

'BUT???' the rest of us ask together.

'But . . . I'm just not sure . . . He's asked me to go to his house next week.'

'To meet his *parents*?'

'Well, maybe,' Mercedes says with that little smile that does-n't show her brace.

'Gosh!' I say, and already I'm thinking about what to wear for the wedding – pink's always nice at a wedding, especially with a pair of spike-heeled pink strappy sandals . . .

'Stop it!' says Mercedes. How does she always know what I'm thinking? 'We're off to make Life Changes with you, Angel, so let's just think about that, shall we?'

We seem to have arrived, so reluctantly I turn my attention back to the gym. What an amazing place! I mean, there is SO much going on. I never realised so many people did this gym thing.

After lots of help from a very shiny, smiley, tanned woman at the reception desk, I decide on yoga and kick-boxing. Yoga, for that calm, well-stretched feeling, and kick-boxing, well, I know it isn't exactly *feminine*, but I decide that the fact that it's mostly boys doing it could be a real plus. Also, the lycra factor involved in both yoga and kick-boxing is low (i.e., I don't have to wear it) and they are both SO toning. Even if it's not worth trying to impress Adam, I still want to be the hostess with the mostest at the Fashion Show. And I want Sydney to realise that I'm not a girl to be trifled with, or teased for that matter. I want him to see that I'm cool and in control.

On our way out we notice a sign saying 'Instant Tanning and Sunbeds', and who do we see sneaking in? Adam.

'Oh, help,' moans Portia, 'I think I'm going to be sick.'

Luckily Adam doesn't see us, but now we all see him for what he really is, a vain, fake-tanned, short-arsed, greaseball . . . and he is *very* short without the high-heeled boots. I would have had to get down on my hands and knees to have a conversation with him.

'Girls, we must MOVE ON,' I say in my most governessy voice. 'It's no good any of us standing here thinking about what might have been.' (I know he's a vain, short-arsed, greaseball, but I still can't help wishing I'd had the chance to tell him that.)

We make our way home. My lovely friends all have their own things to do this afternoon. Portia looks done in, so we suggest she goes home for a rest. Minnie is sewing away at home and Mercedes is going with her to try on some of the things she's made and practise modelling them.

After a light lunch, I go off on my own back to the gym to start my Life Changes with a kick-boxing class, followed by some yoga.

Sydney's squishy section (I wish)

IT'S FAB!!! I really love this! I have an instructor who reminds me of J.O.N.C. (flutter, flutter) and we get to do all sorts amazing things, like a 'cut kick' and a 'spinning back kick'. It's just so exciting, especially when we are taught to 'visually lock on to your target and bury your foot in his abdomen.'

Quite honestly, imagining positioning a swift kick to Sydney's squishy section when he's being a twerp is WONDERFUL. I put everything I've got into my practise kick. The instructor says I'm a 'natural' and he's not talking about my hair colour here. Just think, I've been a kick-boxer all this time without knowing it! He says that having long legs is a real advantage and that I must stand properly and put my weight behind my kicks. Could I have chosen anything better? Suddenly being a giant heffalump is a real advantage. I can already picture myself as Kick-Boxing Champion of the World. I'll have more black belts than Prada.

114

When kick-boxing is over, I make my way to the yoga studio to chill out after a hard workout. Yoga is BLISS. Apart from lying flat on my mat and drifting off while visualising walking along a sun-drenched beach, I have to do some really whacky things. There's the lotus thing (tying your legs up in a knot), the cobra thing (pretending to be a snake – you have to be really bendy to be able to do it properly), a shoulder stand (when you hold your legs in the air and then try to get your feet to touch the floor behind you, which I could ALMOST do . . . I'm so glad I'm not on the Blow Your Mind Cabbage Diet now or this particular move could have been windier than Chicago). Then there's lying flat and breathing. I've certainly never had any problem with lying flat *or* breathing, so I like yoga straight away.

After an hour of trying to knot and unknot various bits of me I am SO chilled out that I can hardly walk. I sort of drift home on a little pink cloud and only just find enough energy to phone the others when I get in.

Minnie and Mercedes are full of their afternoon. Mercedes says that Minnie has made her a fab dress and she's been prac-tising her model walk while smiling without showing her brace. She has also discovered that Paul's uncle runs a really smart catering company and that if I phone him he may be willing to lend us some tables and chairs for the Fashion Show dinner.

'OK, wonderful,' I say, all excited. 'Now what about some tea? Flossie made banana bread last night. Why don't you come round and have some and then we could ring Portia and see if she's all right?'

'OOOOOH, yes please,' says Minnie, and we all know what she's thinking: SUNDAY + ANGEL'S HOUSE + TEA = GEORGE.

We get quite a party going in the sitting room. Mother and Potty and Flossie drink tea together, while George and Portia (who came round wanting to know if Greaseball showed up again at the gym) play Hunt the Twiglet with Stinker. Well, George isn't really *playing*, he's much too strong and silent for that, but he is handing the Twiglets to Portia, which is quite something for him.

Minnie goes into a sort of pale pink swoon watching George, while I get terribly over-excited telling everyone about my afternoon. I demonstrate a few kicks, which makes Potty rather wobbly. 'Steady on, Cherub,' he says. 'Nearly knocked my teeth into my tea!'

'Ooops, sorry,' I say as I go into my version of a full lotus and chant a bit. (The class didn't actually involve any chanting, but I thought it would sound impressive). Meanwhile Minnie is sitting with her chin cupped in her hands, gazing at George who is completely unmoved as he munches his way through his second slice of banana bread. I'm busy doing a wind-free shoulder stand when Mother actually notices me and says that she thinks all this exercise is a 'jolly good idea, dahling. You've inspired me to have a few sessions in the flotation tank myself'.

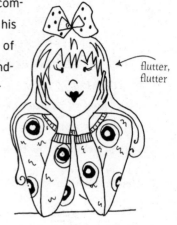

flutter, flutter

'That's hardly exercise,' I snort, and she rather snappily tells me that keeping afloat is much harder work than I would think. Well, maybe if you're just a bag of bones, but I've never had any problem floating.

Potty is also very enthusiastic about the exercise idea and says that he and Stinker might go and practise some netball in the garden.

Flossie tells us that in 'her day' they had to 'either walk on our two flat feet, or pedal on our bikes. None of this gym and flotation stuff for us – lawks no! If you had any energy left by the end of the day you knew you'd forgotten to do something.'

I feel jolly pleased with myself as I totter up to Heaven later. I've made a brilliant Life Change – one that I honestly think I can keep up. I loved the yoga, and as for the kick-boxing, well, Sydney had better beware. One more Slimy Slithering from him and I'll give him a double spinning back kick that he won't forget in a hurry. (Actually, I probably won't . . . but I COULD if I wanted to.)

I've also made huge strides in my catering plans for the Fashion Show. After tea I rang Paul's uncle, who sounded divine, and he said he would do anything he could to help. How brilliant is that?

As I drift off to sleep I think about Mother . . . I suppose she might have been right about the crash diet. Even if I had lost loads of weight I probably would have wodged it all on again as soon as I started eating anything more calorific that cabbage . . .

Fitness Fruit Flollop

1 ripe pear	a pinch of cinnamon
1 tbsp lemon juice	½ a glass of water
1 tbsp honey	

———

Peel and core the pear. Chop it up and squeeze the lemon juice over it. Put the pear with lemon juice, the honey and the cinnamon into a blender or food processor, switch it on and slowly pour in the water as it blends.

Makes a delish, smooth drink, best served straight from the fridge, very, very cold. AMAZINGLY healthy!

chapter fifteen

Committee and Cakes

RATHER EARLY ON Monday morning I open the back door to find Mrs Sophie Something-Hyphenated standing on the doorstep with a cat basket under her arm. Flossie and I go into freeze-frame mode while we wait to hear what her next batty scheme is.

'Flossie,' she says, brushing down her slightly grubby pale blue twin set, 'I'm looking for people to adopt stray cats. I've got the sweetest little moggy here and she just said to me, "Pleeease, it would be *purrrrr*fect to live with Angel and Clarrrrisa next door . . ."' She has put on a nauseating sort of 'pussy cat' voice. '*Dooo* come and have a lickle look at me.' And so saying she opens the basket. Stinker, who has been lying quite happily under the kitchen table until now, is instantly on red alert. He springs, all four feet at once, towards the two fluffy ears that are just showing over the top of the basket. There's a fantastic hullaballoo while the cat scrambles wildly and claws her way over Mrs Something-Hyphenated's shoulder (making her scream with combined shock and agony). The basket goes flying, I fling myself (very bravely) at Stinker and land sprawled across the floor at Mrs Sophie Something-Hyphenated's feet. The cat disappears into the wild blue yonder.

Mrs Something-Hyphenated is still trembling a bit when Stinker escapes my clutches and hurtles through her legs to see if he can catch a mouthful of that scrumptious fur before it leaves Knightsbridge. With that, she crumples into a well-upholstered heap by the back door and Flossie and I have to give her a cup of strong sweet tea before she stops trembling.

Luckily (or unluckily, depending on which way you look at it), she recovers enough to take me to school. The Range Rover smells particularly disgusting, as the stinky children have been festering inside it while the cat saga was going on. (I also suspect that it has been home to a few dozen other stray cats over the last week.) The children are as usual totally nauseating and ask me deeply blush-making questions about the Valentine disco. They want to know if I 'snogged' anyone. I'm feeling so sick of them and the cat pee smell that I launch off into toe-curling detail of my night of endless 'snogging' with at least ten different boys. I have to keep my voice very low in case Mrs Something-

wobbly rose

scaredy cat

cardboard shoes

Hyphenated hears, but, by the time I've finished my 'tonsil cleaning' descriptions, both children are so totally gobsmacked that I have no need for the sticky toffees and I arrive at school feeling mightily pleased with myself.

'Hello, babes,' I say, waltzing into the classroom with my stinky Range Rover victory still fresh in my mind. 'What's going on?' I can hear the throb of a motorbike in the background, but I'm not even going to turn around. Portia, however, looks a bit pale, and Minnie, seeing that all is not well with the poor girl, starts jabbering on about the charity fund raising event.

'Oh, right!' I say, trying to help distract Portia. 'How are your fabulous frocks coming on, Minnie?'

I have to shout the last bit because the boys, Slimy Sydney amongst them, are playing Gladiators with hockey sticks, and wearing boxer shorts on their heads (what strange creatures boys are . . .).

'I've still got quite a lot of sewing to do and I'm not sure any of it's any good, but I'm getting there,' shrieks Minnie. 'What about your foodie plans, Angel?'

I'm taking a deep breath before shouting back my news about Paul's uncle when the Gladiator Spectacular comes to an abrupt end and Ms Worhause shimmies in. (Today, she's wearing shocking pink from head to toe, with clashing orange beads and dangly earrings. And as she sits down there is a flash of her orange- and pink-striped ankle. She's SO cool, and big.)

When everyone has settled down and the 'gladiators' are under control we report our progress with the Fashion Show plans to Ms Worhause.

When I phoned Paul's uncle last night, he said he would lend us, free of charge, really glam tables and chairs (little gold ones), beautiful white linen cloths, and all the cutlery and glasses. I can't wait to tell Ms Worhause how totally brill I've been.

With a twinkle of her dangly earrings Ms Worhause says, 'Now I would like a spokesperson for the fund-raising committee to update me on their progress.'

Portia stands up, but it's no good, I *have* to tell everyone my news or I'll burst. 'I've been promised twenty tables, a hundred and sixty chairs, white linen cloths and all the cutlery and glasses for FREE!!'

'Well done, Angel!' says Ms Worhause and there's a flutter around the room of people saying, 'Wow!' and 'Fantastic!' and 'Genius!'. I'm just so PINK with pleasure that I start rattling off what I'm going to cook (with the help of J.O.N.C. – boom, boom, boom).

When Portia finally has a chance to speak, she says that somebody's uncle's second cousin twice removed (or something like that) is Jasper Conran, and that he is going to lend us one of his couture evening dresses, worth about one thousand pounds! Portia's kept really quiet about this so it comes as a complete surprise and we all clap and cheer.

Then Minnie gives us an update on her little collection of groovy gear, but says she's getting a bit bogged down because she's got loads of ideas but not that much time now to finish them (we've only got four weeks to go).

'This all sounds very exciting,' says Ms Worhause. 'May I suggest that you organise your models and start rehearsals, at every possible break, as soon as possible? You don't need to have all the clothes here before you begin to work out the music and which boys are going to accompany which girls on the catwalk.'

I still think boys modelling might be a mistake. Let's hope Ms Worhause will help us organise the pathetic creatures. Then suddenly I feel a bit nervous and whisper to Portia, 'Will people have to see me?'

'Of course they'll have to see you, silly. You'll be showing them where to sit and helping them find the buffet table and generally being lovely, just like you always are.'

Oh, flattery can get you anywhere. 'All right,' I say. 'Just so long as I can wear black from head to toe and blend into the background.'

'You'll have to be at all the rehearsals so you know when everything's happening,' says Portia.

'Oh, of course I'll come to rehearsals – I don't want to miss ANYTHING.' Honestly, I'm getting so excited about it all.

Mercedes turns around to say that she's feeling horribly nervous too and does she really *have* to be a model?

'Don't be silly,' says Minnie, 'you can't *not* be a model. You're going to be the Naomi Campbell of our fabulous fashion evening.' (But Mercedes will behave better, natch.) It takes us quite a long time to convince Mercedes that her brace doesn't feature at all when she does her dead sophisticated, closed-lip smile. It's funny, isn't it, what people worry about? I mean, if I had Mercedes's amazing figure, would I worry about a piffling little brace? NO I WOULD NOT. But then I wouldn't think that I wasn't talented or that people wouldn't always really like me if I was Minnie. And I certainly wouldn't worry if I had one or two TINY pimples if I was Portia. I wonder why we all worry about the things we think are wrong with us instead of trying to think about our good points – funny that.

There's a sort of flurry and a whiff of Miss Dior and the scintillating Scarlet appears. 'Don't crowd me,' she trills as she whooshes in through the door and air-kisses Vivi. I'm sure she's always late just so she can make an entrance.

'God, what a journey I had this morning, getting to school,' she gushes. 'There were so many people around this morning.

125

Minnie says her mouth looks like a gorrilla's bottom – nice!

hip thrusting model walk – pathetic!

Daddy simply couldn't get the Rolls through.'

'Someone must have leaked the news that you were going to be in the area,' says Portia, with *heavy* sarcasm.

But the sarcasm is completely lost on Scarlet. 'That's just what I was thinking, although I do, of course, always come that way to school. But maybe word got out that I was approached by yet another film producer . . .'

'Whatever,' says Portia, while the rest of us groan inwardly. 'The thing is, Scarlet, that you've missed most of our charity fund-raising meeting.'

'Oh, oops, silly me. I'd *completely* forgotten that was happening this morning, what with all the excitement of being discovered yet again. What's going on? *Do* tell.' With that she sits down and throws her hair about a bit before giving us her 'Gosh I'm interested' look.

This Fashion Show is going to be sublime,' she oozes. 'Where are the clothes coming from? Dior, Chanel, Prada?' (Doesn't she ever listen to *anything* that's going on?)

'Well, maybe not,' says Portia. 'Minnie, as you know, is designing and making some of the clothes.'

Here Scarlet looks a bit doubtful so Portia adds, 'Which she is BRILLIANT at.'

'Oh, I know *that*,' says Scarlet.

'But I do really need some help. There's still so much left to do,' says Minnie again.

'If you wanted some help, my darling cousin is at St Martin's doing fashion design and I'm sure that if I asked her she would come and give you a hand, Minnie.'

Minnie looks really delighted, so for once Miss 'I think I'm a Superstar' Scarlet has been of some help.

'We've borrowed lots of clothes from other shops . . .' says Portia.

'Not Chanel or Prada?' asks Scarlet with her forehead all puckered up like a festoon blind.

'Well, maybe,' says Portia. 'If *you* want to go and ask them . . .'

'I easily could,' boasts Scarlet. 'Daddy and Mummy shop there *all* the time.'

'You try that, then,' says Portia.

Suddenly Scarlet realises that maybe she's been a teensy bit rash and adds, 'Of course, I'm going to be *frightfully* busy. I just may not have time.'

'Well anyway,' says Portia, 'we're making clothes, some boutiques are lending us clothes and we've been promised a Jasper Conran evening dress. When it arrives we'll need to choose someone to model it.'

'Model a Jasper *Conran*?' shrieks Scarlet. 'OF COURSE I'll do it.' Did anyone ask her? 'I've had so much experience modelling. I'll be able to show you all how to walk properly down the catwalk.'

'Oh GOODY,' says Mercedes.

Once again the sarcasm misses its target and Scarlet beams at us all. 'When shall we begin?' she asks.

It's been a really heavy day with all our organising and planning, but I'll be able to unwind at kick-boxing class this evening. I need to feel fit and strong for my catering and hostessing duties. I've been looking forward to it all day. Every time I see Slimy Sydney I feel really smug because he doesn't know that if he's grotty to me *one more* time, I could flatten him with a rear leg kick. When he told me today that he thought it was a 'HUGE' shame that I wasn't going to be a model, with that slimy smile of his, I could just picture myself leaving him in horrible agony with my footprint in his stomach. A divine picture.

chapter sixteen

Spots, Sydney . . . SUICIDE!

THE FASHION SHOW is fast approaching and Flossie is being so brilliant about the food. We've spent hours together, searching through recipe books (with J.O.N.C. still being the hot, top favourite) and we've found wondrous things to fill the fashion-conscious with. Nothing too heavy, though – you don't

want to feel like a plum pudding when you're watching tiny souf-flés wafting down the catwalk. We've planned and shopped and cooked and frozen, and gosh, I've been so busy, what with all this foodie stuff, the kick-boxing, the yoga and all the rehearsals. A girl's barely got time to EXFOLIATE these days!

Potty has been very busy too, with his pamphlets, the latest being 'How to Speak Martian'. He's terribly pleased with this one. 'Must be able to talk to the blighters when they land, Cherub. Otherwise one could put one's foot in it without really realising.' How true.

Mother seems to be spending more and more time floating, which means that we don't see her for hours on end – not that we ever saw her much anyway, but now when she does appear she looks all pale and interesting, as if she's been locked away in a cupboard for days. Which I suppose is exactly where she has been.

From the kitchen window I can see Mrs Sophie Something-Hyphenated plodding down the steps to the back door. She looks a bit anxious as I let her in, and I see her glancing under the kitchen table. I expect she's worried that Stinker might be about to pounce again, but I'm pretty sure that he's much too busy digging up the plants that Diggory has just planted in the garden, to bother with someone who hasn't got a cat basket.

'I wondered whether Clarissa would be interested in a little recycling project that I'm working on?' Flossie and I both look from Mrs Something-Hyphenated's worried face to her hand, where she's clutching what looks suspiciously like a fistful of Potty's pamphlets.

I'm afraid Mrs Cookson Potts isn't at home at the moment,' says Flossie. 'But I will ask her as soon as she comes in.'

'Oh good, Flossie,' Mrs Something-Hyphenated replies. 'I'm so keen for all this rubbish,' (here she waves Potty's pamphlets around), 'to be made into something useful.'

'Yes, of course,' says Flossie, keeping a completely straight face.

We think we've got through Mrs Something-Hyphenated's visit fairly successfully when Stinker saunters in from his excavations in the garden. He's covered in mud and there's a smell of something not too yummy about him. He's a very kind-hearted dog, if a little bonkers, and he notices that Mrs Something-Hyphenated is looking unhappy (actually, it's the sight of him that's made her look so miserable, but Stinker doesn't know that). He proceeds full-tilt towards her so that he can wrap himself affectionately around her polyester-covered legs and give her a thoroughly good licking. She screams, this time with a mixture of horror and disgust, which just makes Stinker try that much harder with the wrapping and the licking. Mrs Something-Hyphenated backs out of the kitchen door as quickly

how could she possibly prefer her stinky children to Stinker himself?

trying SO hard to be friendly

as she can while trying to shake Stinker off. She only just manages to close the door, leaving Stinker on one side and her thick polyester legs on the other, but she drops all Potty's pamphlets on the way. We wait for a minute to see if she'll come back for them, but funnily enough, she doesn't.

I'm really not upset in the least when Mrs Something-Hyphenated goes on and on the next morning about keeping animals under control and the dangers of rabies. Even her icky children don't bother me with their poo jokes and embarrassing questions about what it feels like to have boobs.

Everything is going *so* well. Flossie and I are beginning to fill the freezers with fabby dabby food for the Fashion Show. We've made quiches and salmon *en croute*, jubilee chicken, homemade rolls and all sorts of puddings. And I'm feeling full of girl power and good vibes from my sessions at the gym.

The rehearsals for the show have been going really well too. Some of the boys have *even* been helpful! The catwalk was finished about a week ago and Sydney (big surprise) was brilliant at helping to put it all together. Minnie tells me that I'm mean to him and that he only says the things he does because he's trying to be funny. But as we know she can be totally bonkers sometimes.

Anyway, she is doing incredibly well with her 'collection' now that Scarlet's cousin (who isn't a *bit* like Scarlet, thank goodness) is helping.

We've only got four days to go until the show and it's been brilliant fun to watch my friends practising their modelly walks. (I had a go when no one else was around – it feels SCARY being up there on that catwalk.) Scarlet has bagged the Jasper Conran dress, of course, and Sydney is going to escort her down the catwalk. I have to admit that he's a much better model than Scarlet and actually looks quite good. From a distance, with your eyes half closed.

When I arrive at school the others are already there. 'Look at these amazing things Minnie's made for the show!' Mercedes enthuses.

'Wow, Minnie, you must have used about a zillion sequins on this one,' I say, holding up a *gorgeoise* T-shirt that Minnie has decorated in a sixties style with sparkly flowers. She's also made about two dozen skirts, twenty decorated T-shirts, lots of her speciality beanie hats, belts and little beaded bags.

While we're getting excited about all her wonderful clothes, the door to the classroom opens. The whiff of Miss Dior is there, but the flurry is definitely missing. Scarlet stands stock still in the doorway (this is called 'making an entrance'), and she waits until we have all stopped talking and are looking her way. She's wrapped in a black pashmina and is wearing those stupid sunglasses again – honestly anything for effect.

'Oooh,' she whispers. 'Oooh.' Louder this time, until someone pretty much has to ask her, 'What's the matter, Scarlet?'

'*Ooooohh*, I'm *so* unwell. I just want to be alone . . .' With this, she flings her pashmina dramatically over her shoulder and walks to her desk as if she's holding an egg between her knees. 'Ooohh,' she says again as she sits down.

'Ooh, for goodness' sake,' says Portia. 'What *is* the matter, Scarlet, and how "unwell" are you?'

spot the spot

groaning
a bit

Very slowly, Scarlet unwraps the scarf from around her face and takes off her sunglasses. I'll say this for her: she certainly knows how to hold an audience. 'Look,' she says in her most 'I'm a tragic heroine' voice. We crowd around, we look . . . and yes, there it is – A SPOT. Well, to be perfectly disgusting about it, it's more of a *pustule* actually, bordering on a *boil*.

'For goodness' sake, Scarlet,' says Portia. 'You don't have to go into hiding because you've got *one* spot.' And here she rather anxiously touches her own face because she feels spots are her speciality.

Scarlet whimpers, 'There's only one on my *face* . . .'

'Are there others somewhere else?' I ask.

'Yes,' she sighs, 'there are some on my body.'

We all crowd around to get a proper look while Scarlet moans softly. 'Blimey,' says Sydney. 'I recognise those spots. She's got CHICKENPOX.'

I know it's mean, but I'm afraid rather a lot of us laugh – I mean, *chickenpox* for goodness' sake. Most of us had chickenpox when were were five, not fourteen! Some of the boys, who shall remain nameless, start strutting around the room clucking, and one even goes all broody, sitting on a football in the corner. I have to say I do feel a bit sorry for Scarlet. She must

134

be feeling so grotty. But I'm sure she only came into school for the dramatic effect. If anyone deserves to fall flat on their spotty little face, it's Scarlet.

Vivi takes Scarlet off to the san, where they call her father to come and collect her (in the Rolls) and we are left to explain to Ms Worhause what has happened.

'It was *amazing*,' Sydney enthuses. 'Spots were just popping out all over the place.' (Slight exaggeration, but it was quite alarming.)

'Good gracious!' exclaims Ms Worhause (who is in daffodil yellow from head to toe with green, purple and turquoise beads, and lots of red lipstick on her acrobatic mouth). 'This is devastating news. Wasn't Scarlet going to model the superb evening gown lent to us by Jasper Conran?' Crumbs! I'd almost forgotten that she'd bagged the star of the show. We'll have to find someone else to model.

'Right, committee members,' says Ms Worhause, 'would you come with me, please? The rest of you get on with your English essays. We shall be back in a few minutes.'

We follow the whoosh of yellow down the corridor. We reach the dressing rooms behind the stage and Ms Worhause beckons us in. She goes to the

this is a DRESS?? looks like barbies underwear to me

135

clothes rails and comes back with the *incredible* dress over her arm. It's all strappy and narrow and low at the front – gosh, it must show almost all a girl's got. Minnie tells us we shouldn't worry because it's cut on the cross (whatever that means), so although it looks skinny on the hanger, it would actually fit almost anyone.

'Committee members, you must now select another model for this wonderful dress,' says Ms Worhause.

In a split second, six voices (there are only eight of us altogether) exclaim, 'ANGEL!'

WHAT?? You could hear the 'clunk' as my jaw hit the floor. 'But it will NEVER fit me!'

'Yes, Angel, it will. It *must* be you who models it,' says Minnie (who used to be my friend). 'You've watched all the rehearsals and you know how to do the walk and when to come on and everything. It will expand widthwise, which will only make it a bit shorter. It was really too long for Scarlet anyway – she was going to have to hold it up as she walked. And I can't take up the hem because of the gorgeous beads and sequins all round the bottom. Honestly, Angel, it will only work on a tall girl, and you and Scarlet are the tallest girls – and you are at least half a head taller even than Scarlet.'

'But I'm being a hostess.'

'That's all right, there'll be plenty of time to nip backstage and change – this dress comes on last.'

'Why can't one of the others model it?' I whimper.

'That's what I've just explained, Angel,' says Minnie patiently. 'There is no one else tall enough, and anyway, everyone except Scarlet is doing the big group scene just before the Jasper Conran dress comes on, and there wouldn't be time to get one of the other models into the dress.' Now she's smiling. 'Sydney will escort you down the catwalk, kiss you at the end and then escort you back again, so you barely have to do anything other than smile.'

I splutter. I gasp. I groan. I go pink from head to toe. 'I CAN'T. Minnie, you know I can't,' I finally wail. 'Ms Worhause, I CAN'T. I mean, look at me. Look at that dress . . . and Sydney. NO, oh no, PLEEEASE, no.'

All the other committee members start piping up. 'You'll *have* to do it, Angel. We haven't time to rehearse anyone else.'

'If you don't do it, the whole show will be ruined.'

'We NEED you.'

'You'll look lovely.'

'You *will* do it, won't you?' Minnie pleads. 'All our hard work will have been for nothing if you say no.' Everybody looks at me imploringly.

What can I say? I just sit with my mouth open, sort of shivering. Ms Worhause smiles sweetly at me and, as she turns to hang the dress back up, she says, 'Don't worry, Angel, you'll be absolutely fine. Now that's settled. We will have a fitting tomorrow, first thing, so you don't need to even think about it before then.' And with that, she swishes out of the room.

I'm dazed. Did that really happen? No, it couldn't have. My friends *couldn't* have said that I would have to wear *that*, that . . . that not-quite-all-there dress. My knickers are bigger than that! I see stars. Surely I'm going to faint now? All those people looking at me . . . all my wobbly bits on display . . . I can't do it! *Everything* will show in that dress. I'll look like a whale. A whale with beads and sequins! I'll probably burst the seams and bits of me will come squodging out like sausage meat. But how can I say no to my very, very best friends? And I *can't* kiss Sydney – the words 'kiss' and 'Sydney' just don't go together. I'd rather kiss Stinker's bottom than kiss Sydney . . .

MY LIFE IS IN RUINS.

chapter seventeen

Soggy Hankies and Syrup of Figs

IT'S NO GOOD. Nothing's going to help. I've pleaded with Ms Worhause, but she won't budge. She says Minnie is right, there just isn't anyone else who could do it and it would be too big a loss to leave the dress out of the show altogether. It feels as though someone keeps kicking me in the stomach and there is *nothing* I can do to stop them.

Even my Wednesday evening yoga class doesn't help. When we do the 'visualise yourself walking along a beach' bit, all I can see is my big, wobbly, out-of-control body falling out of that dress as I shuffle down the catwalk. I think I'll just go home and DIE.

'Flossie!' I wail as I come in through the kitchen door. 'Flossie, I'm going to die now. Goodbye.'

'Whatever is the matter with you, my girl?'

'Flossie, my life is so over. I'm going to go to sleep and NEVER wake up.'

'Now, now,' says Flossie. 'What you need is a jolly good purge. I thought you looked a bit peaky at breakfast – you just wait while I get the Syrup of Figs . . .'

I haven't even got the energy to argue about the Syrup of Figs. I just sit in a huge, helpless heap and hardly even notice when Minnie, Mercedes and Portia arrive.

not a pretty sight – even my hair's depressed

'Angel, we're worried about you. You've hardly spoken since the meeting,' says Minnie.

'You look all washed up,' adds Mercedes.

'I *am* all washed up – *and* down the plughole,' I say.

'It can't be *that* bad, can it?' asks Portia.

'Yes,' I reply, 'it CAN.'

Flossie comes back with the Syrup of Figs and offers everyone a spoonful. The others, funnily enough, refuse. But I just drink the beastly stuff anyway. What does anything matter now? I might just as well drink poison for all I care.

Minnie tries to reassure me. 'It won't be nearly as bad as you think.'

'Yes it will,' I say.

'Now, what is all this nonsense about?' asks Flossie.

'They are MAKING me model a dress that's no bigger than one of your dusters and I have *to kiss* Sydney,' I whine.

'And there was me thinking it was something serious,' she says as she opens up the biscuit tin, full of beautiful Pecan Puffs (made before my life ended).

'If this isn't serious, then I don't know what is,' I say.

'Well,' says Flossie, 'someone being very under the weather or dead even – *that* would be serious.' She fetches a plate of fruit bread, spread with unsalted butter.

'Well, Scarlet's "under the weather",' I snap, and *I'm* dead.' Now I really am sobbing and it's not pretty either. It's that awful sort of snotty sobbing that once you've started you can't stop.

Mercedes comes and puts her arms around me and the others crowd around and make comforting noises.

'You'll look wonderful,' says Portia. 'That's why we want you to do it.' Which just makes me sob even louder.

'And Sydney's not *so* bad,' says Mercedes. 'I think he's rather gorgeous, actually. I mean, you might have had to kiss *Adam*.'

That's it. The floodgates are open. I know I shouldn't feel so sorry for myself, but I can't help it. Just weeks ago I was a happy, food-loving girl, who fancied a boy in the Upper Sixth with a big red (throbbing) bike. Now I'm left with no dream lover, no life, no hope, just a few straps, a whisper of cloth, Sydney and the prospect of TOTAL humiliation in front of EVERYONE.

While I'm busy flooding the kitchen, Potty and Stinker come in. (Potty's wearing his wig and gown so he's probably been gardening.) 'Little Cherub,' Potty says to me, 'what's all this? Not been watching *Magic Roundabout* again, have you?'

'No,' I sob. 'My life is OVER. I have to be a model and kiss Sydney.'

And he says, 'Could be worse. Could be off to wrestle a lion. Now *that* would be a worry.'

I can see his point, but it doesn't make me feel much better.

Stinker has been back into the garden and now appears with an old sock of mine, which he must have buried somewhere and which he has now thoughtfully dug up again for me. I'm so touched when he puts the smelly old thing in my lap that I start to sob again.

Potty paces up and down looking worried. 'Tell you what – why don't I go and write a pamphlet for you? Spiffing idea. I shall call it "How to Feel Happy – Look in the Mirror and Say 'I'm Wonderful!'" You should try it, Cherub. Telling yourself you're wonderful can really make you smile, and what could be nicer than that?' With that, he bustles off and I'm left considering the idea, which has at least taken my mind off the other thing for a while. Of course, Mother is nowhere to be found. I don't expect she would care if I had to model naked in front of the whole school.

George drifts in while I'm mopping up and Minnie takes great delight in whispering into his ear what the problem is. Even when I'm a complete WRECK she doesn't miss a chance to get as close as she can to George. Today, he's looking distinctly rumpled and I suspect that 'study-leaving' has in fact meant sleeping on the sofa in front of the telly all day. 'Don't worry, Angel,' he says. 'You'll be great.'

'I *know* I'll be GREAT. That's the whole problem,' I groan. 'I'll be a *great* big gallumphing whale in a teeny-weeny, itsy-bitsy THING, that doesn't cover *anything* it should.'

George is unfazed. I suppose he's used to me by now. 'I expect you'll be the Face of the Future.'

'It's not my FACE I'm worried about,' I snarl.

I mean, how close do you have to be to whisper to someone?

I plucked his eyebrows for him when he was 12

'Silly girl,' says Flossie. 'Have a nice slice of fruit bread and behave yourself.'

I don't often do this, but something just goes PING (no, *not* my knicker elastic), and I get up, sniff loudly and STOMP out of the room, slamming the door really effectively behind me.

Once I'm up in Heaven on my own I can think about the full awfulness of what has happened. MOST awful of all is that I don't seem to be dead and other than being dead I don't see how I'm going to get out of this . . . There's a tap at the door – it's probably the gorgeous girlies, I think. Come to rescue me. So I go to let them in and find, to my amazement, that *Mother* is standing there. What can she be doing? That's twice in two months! She must have taken a wrong turn on the stairs and come up here by mistake.

'Hello,' I say, trying to stop my nose from running.

'Hello, dahling,' she replies.

'Are you all right?' I ask her.

'Yes, perfectly, dahling. But a little bird tells me that maybe *you* are not all right?' Gosh, whichever 'little bird' it was worked jolly fast and must have made a big impression on Mother, who is looking at me with what I can only describe as 'motherliness'. I'm so goggled by this that I forget, for a moment, that my world has fallen apart and just stare at her immaculately made-up face. 'Shall I come in?' she asks.

'Oh yes,' I say, and with that she glides in and sits herself down on my pink duvet.

'Now, dahling, tell me all about it.'

That's all it takes for the floodgates to open again and with a WHOOSH, the whole panic-making story comes out. I hear myself telling Mother that I feel like a fat ugly freak and that all my friends are tiny and beautiful and look as if they've stepped out of glossy magazines . . . that I'm only really any good at cooking and that I was so happy to be doing the food for the Fashion Show, but that now they're MAKING me model this teeny-weeny dress and that I'll look like a vast blob and make her even more ashamed of me than she is already, and that I've got to kiss Sydney who calls me Jelly Potts and teases me and is the last person in the entire universe that I want to kiss, and that everyone is ganging up on me and won't let me get out of it and that I WISH I WAS DEAD.

I didn't think there could be any more salt water in me, but somehow I've managed to dredge up more tears. Luckily this time they're not quite so snotty (which I don't think Mother would have liked much). She produces a little lace hanky and I dab it around my face a bit before she says, 'Dahling, I've been meaning to talk to you for a while now.'

I'm just wondering why she *hasn't* talked to me if she's been meaning to, and also whether it's going to be a 'gallumphing' lecture again, which WILL NOT HELP, when she says, 'What we really need to do is to get you the proper *underpinnings*.'

What is she talking about? I thought 'underpinning' was something you did to a house. I'm sure Mercedes's grandparents had to have their house underpinned . . . Does Mother mean that I need to move out of my bedroom? 'What do you mean?' I ask, my voice still a bit trembly from all the tears.

'Underpinnings, dahling. Underthings . . . You know – we need to get you properly fitted for a *bra*.'

I gulp. 'Oh.'

'It doesn't matter how wonderful the clothes are, dahling, NOTHING looks good on a girl unless she's got the under garments right, and that means spending some time being properly fitted. Once you've got the *right* underpinnings, everything else will fall into place.' Even I can see the joke here and we have a proper mumsy–daughter giggle together.

Much later on, after I've watched six back-to-back episodes of *Buffy* and eaten as much ice cream as is sensible, I lie tucked up in Heaven and think about the day. Will something as tiny (well, *huge* in my case) as a bra make a difference? Could Mother be right again, like she was about the crash diet?

It's amazing, really. At tea-time the end of the world was nigh and now here's Mother offering to take me to Horrids and *buy* me things. I can't even remember when I last went shopping with Mother. It used to be Flossie who chose my smocked dresses and OshKosh dungarees and now here is my own mother offering to come and choose underpinnings. Well, that's better than a smack in the eye with a wet fish, isn't it?, as Flossie would say.

Spirit-Lifting, Yummy Homemade Fudge

100g butter　　*1 cup of ordinary milk*
900g caster sugar　*a few drops of vanilla*
1 tin of condensed　　*extract*
　milk (400g)

Put all the ingredients into a saucepan and cook over a gentle heat until the sugar and butter have melted, then bring to the boil. Boil (not too hard) for 15 minutes-ish stirring all the time (it will be worth it). As soon as the mixture starts to look sugary and begins to come away from the sides of the pan, it is time to stop and pour it into a 3cm x 20cm roasting tin to set. The other way of seeing whether it's ready is to spoon a little out on to a saucer and see if it sets. If it doesn't, you can lick that off and try again a few minutes later.

When it's cold cut it into squares and ENJOY!

chapter eighteen

An Uplifting Experience

THERE IT IS, still looming, the ghastly grizzly prospect of the dress and Sydney, to say nothing of the KISS. Even the thought of shopping after school with Mother isn't making it seem any less horrific.

I plod through the day like a zombie, still secretly hoping that an alien spaceship may whisk me away before the *you-know-what*. I must speak to Portia, who's always dreaming about alien spaceships, if she knows a way to get me into a different universe before it's too late.

Luckily no one mentions the *you-know-what* during the day and even Sydney seems to be avoiding me. When I get home Mother is already waiting, Louis Vuitton clutch bag in hand. She goes on waiting, very patiently, while I change out of my designer (not) uniform and have a little something to stop my tummy rumbling.

'Now, have you put on something that's easy to take off?' Mother asks when I'm finally ready.

'Oh golly! Am I going to have to take my clothes off?' I ask her, feeling a bit goofy.

She laughs. 'Dahling, it would be terribly hard to buy a bra without taking *some* clothes off, don't you think?'

Well, no, I didn't think, because usually when the gorgeous girlies and I go on shopping trips for frilly things, I just scoop up whatever I think might go around me, pay and come home. Admittedly, sometimes when I get home there are parts of me that prefer not to be encased in nylon lace and that go off and do their own thing. But I really wasn't thinking that I would have to take my clothes off to buy a bra. Help! Perhaps I'm not so keen on this shopping trip idea after all . . .

Mother, however, is not going to be put off – she's got a will of iron. Well, she'd have to have, wouldn't she, to be married to Potty? She takes my hand and almost drags me down the road towards Harrods and The Bra.

Before I even have time to think about whether this might be a good moment for my first proper fainting fit, Mother has got me into the lift and whisked me up to the Lingerie department. I've never been in this bit of Harrods before. I thought at first it said Lingering Department when we reached the right floor, and I had visions of Harrods having a whole department just for people to stand about in.

Suddenly we're surrounded by oceans of sugar-coloured flimsy things with the occasional naughty black or leopard-skin print peeping out from between sensible nighties.

Mother goes and chats to someone behind the counter who looks as if she was born wearing a corset. The woman turns to look at me and smiles (pityingly, probably) before she comes over and says, 'Good afternoon. Would you like to follow me, please?'

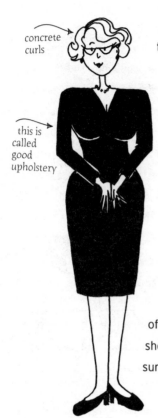

concrete curls

this is called good upholstery

Mrs Born-in-a-Corset

Well, no, is what I want to say, but there's something sort of head-mistressy about her, so I follow like a timid lamb to the changing room. Once we're in there, she whisks a tape measure out of her pocket and tells me to take off my shirt. A tape measure?? Nobody mentioned tape measures . . . I thought she'd just look at me and say, 'Oh yes, you're a size Totally Huge, which you'll find over there.' But not a bit of it. She stands there LOOKING while I take off my shirt, and without even asking she's wrapped the jolly old tape measure around . . . well, I'll just say around the top of me and then again a little bit lower down.

I'm quite pleased that she doesn't pass out from shock when she looks at the measurements. Instead, she says, 'Wonderful,' and vanishes. Wonderful? She must just have meant it was wonderful that she had enough tape measure to go around.

She's back again before I've really had time to notice that there are mirrors all around this cubicle and I can see bits of me that I didn't know *existed*, let alone what shape they were. 'I'll leave you with these to try on first,' she says 'to see if we've got the size right.' And with that she disappears again.

Obviously she hasn't got the size right. One of these bras has what look like ropes and pulleys to keep it up, and another is big enough to *camp* in; in fact, it looks just like a couple of wigwams. I'm just wondering whether you could cut a hole at the top of one of the wigwams for the smoke from the cooking fire to go through when Mrs Born-in-a-Corset pops her head in and asks how I'm doing. I'm not *doing* anything except worrying about whether the curtain fits over the doorway of this changing room properly and she very sweetly asks me if I would like some help. In a blinding flash I realise she means would I like her *in here with me* when I take my very friendly, if a shade small, Top Shop bra off. 'N-N-No, thank you,' I manage shakily. 'I was just choosing which to try first.'

She smiles. 'May I suggest *this* one?' she says, holding up the ropes and pulleys.

I gulp. 'Oh, yes, all right.'

I wait for her to leave. After I've made *quite* sure that there aren't *any* gaps at all around the curtain, I wrestle myself into the gigantic double hammock. Just in time, as Mrs Born-in-a-Corset is suddenly there again, LOOKING at me, and IT.

She fiddles about a bit with it and asks, 'How does that feel?'

'Humungous,' I say, still gasping a bit from the effort of getting it on.

'You're filling the cups quite nicely,' she says. What does she mean? Is that possible? 'Why don't you try this one?' she says, holding up the wigwams. And with that, she's off again.

'Madonna, eat your heart out,' is all I can say when I've got myself into the wigwams. It's like that pointy bra thing she did, but a little more like two church steeples strapped to my front. As for sexy? I'd be sexier in a life jacket.

After Mrs Born-in-a-Corset has popped in and out again a few more times (just to keep me on my toes, I suspect) and left me with a few more gigantic 'underpinnings' (I can see now why Mother calls them 'underpinnings' – most of these con-traptions *could* hold up a house), she finally arrives with a big smile and a handful of gorgeous creamy lace.

'Now that we've got the size right, why don't you try this?' she suggests. 'Perhaps the others are a little, shall we say, *mature* for you? I think you'll prefer this.'

Off she goes again and when I look at the bra that she's brought me, I start to feel that she might be my new best friend. I'm almost certain it won't fit because it's just too pret-ty, but to my surprise, I'm in. I'm so excited, I shout, 'I'm in! I'm in! I've got it on! It fits!'

Both Mrs Born-in-a-Corset and Mother arrive as I fling back the curtain, ready to show every shopper in Harrods my beautiful new bra.

'Well, look at that,' says Mother, smiling. 'It looks absolutely perfect.'

'And what a wonderful cleavage it's given Madam,' says Mrs B-in-a-C.

Cleavage? I whizz around to look in the mirror. There it is, in amongst the lightly wired, unpadded perfection of my beautiful bra – drop-dead gorgeous CLEAVAGE. All those bits of me that escaped and flolloped around my old bra are safely and snugly tucked in and nothing is flollopping at *all*.

I'm much too busy bending and twisting and turning in front of the mirror looking at this whole new me to notice that Mrs B-in-a-C has gone off again. But suddenly she's back, offering me a pair of matching knickers 'with a control panel in the front'. Although this sounds like something in an aeroplane, I pull them on over my Marks & Spencer sensible, draught-free, thick white numbers, and find that the control panel does something *magical* to my not-quite-as-flat-as-it-might-be stomach. Even over the big white pants, these knickers are BRILLIANT! They skim and slim and make me feel just DIVINE. Mother, who has managed to find a huge pile of wispy bits and pieces for herself, asks me if I'd like to wear my new treasures home, and what about the same style in other colours? Well, as Sydney would say, 'My cup runneth over,' but I don't mean it quite in the way he does.

I float home, feeling the lovely lacy things hugging me gently under my clothes with a carrier bag containing oceans of tissue paper and three other sets in other colours. Honestly, I could have hugged that Mrs Born-in-a-Corset; in fact, now I think about it, perhaps I did. I certainly hugged Mother and we went home feeling we'd been 'bonded' by bra straps.

'So . . . how did it go?' asks Flossie when I bounce into the kitchen.

'Oh, Flossie, it was TERRIBLE to start with. I mean, there was this woman and she used a *tape measure* on me – and you know how I'm allergic to tape measures – and then I was never sure when she was going to burst in. I mean, I might have been NAKED or anything. And she brought me these enormous contraptions that would have fitted the Millennium Dome – it was just sooo embarrassing!'

'Goodness me,' says Flossie. 'What a lot of fuss over a vest and pants.'

'Oh no, not a vest and pants – look!' I say and I'm just about to rip my shirt open to show Flossie my totally wicked cleavage and the surrounding lace when George appears in the doorway. I decide that although I do know him very well, perhaps flashing my underwear in the kitchen is going a bit far, so instead, because I'm feeling so gorgeously glam (and not thinking about you-know-when), I decide that finally the moment has come to take George aside and ask him what he's going to do about Minnie.

'Minnie?' he asks, looking puzzled. 'Minnie who?'

'George,' I say, 'for goodness' sake, you must know who Minnie is. She's my beautiful little friend who's round here all the time because you're always on study leave or leaving your studies or whatever it is you're doing here and she wants to see you.'

'Why does she want to see me?'

Honestly, he's being so thick. 'Because she thinks you're fab for some reason, and she would like to spend some time with you,' I explain as patiently as I can.

'Angel,' he says, looking all mournful. 'You must know by now why I spend so much time here . . . To see . . . um . . . er . . . you. I come here to see you. It's you I want to see, not Mickey or whoever.'

Big pause while I try to take this in. 'Oh! Um, gosh, I think I might just go and lie down for a bit; it's been SUCH a busy day and I've got masses of homework and I need to unpack my shopping . . .' I waffle on as I try to think what to say next. This can't be right. I mean, he's like my brother. We used to dig up worms together and have bug races . . . and anyway, this is ME! Wobbly old me . . . Oh my God – can this be an effect of my amazing new underpinnings already? 'Th . . . Thank you, George,' I say. 'Um, see you soon . . .' And I back out of the door and scuttle up the stairs.

I close the door to Heaven. Well, *that's* going to take some thinking about. GOLLY . . . I had no idea George felt like that. I do hope I haven't hurt his feelings. It was just such a surprise . . . he must have noticed that I'm not exactly gorgeous. Perhaps it's because I make him laugh and give him chocolate cake . . . ?

But I can't think about this right now. I've got to bite the bullet. Face the music (and Sydney) and do this HORRIBLE Fashion Show.

chapter nineteen

Full-Frontal Fashion

THE FREAKY FROCK fitting jolly nearly ended in tears (mine). Obviously I kept my eyes shut for the whole horrible business. Even the THOUGHT of that dress, and then the thought of my body, and then the thought of that dress and my body TOGETH-ER is enough to make a girl need therapy. So there I was with my eyes tight shut (hoping my mascara wouldn't smudge) when Minnie, who was doing the fitting, suddenly said, 'Angel, I don't think you can wear that bra . . .'

Well, I can tell you, the only thing about to *fit* at that stage was me. I was on the verge of rolling about on the floor, screaming, 'NO! No you can't make me do it without my beauti-ful, lightly wired, cream lace boob beautifier . . .' Then Minnie continued. 'The straps are the wrong colour – you haven't got a *black* bra, have you?' YES! Yes, thank you, Mother, Mrs Born-in-a-Corset and Mr H.A. Rods – I *have* got a black bra.

'Oh, that's brill, Angel. That'll do fine,' said Minnie.

'Can I turn round?' I ask.

'Of course you can turn round; why wouldn't you be able to?'

'You mean you've managed to do the . . . the . . .' (I can't bring myself to say the word *dress*) '. . . this THING up?' I gasp.

'Yes, of course it's done up, Angel,' said Minnie, in what I thought was rather a sort of long-suffering voice.

'Great,' I say. 'Well, please get it undone as quick as poss and get me out of it before I develop sequinitis and rip it to shreds.'

'You really look wonderful,' whispered Minnie.

'Fibber,' I whispered back.

So that was it, fitting over, selective amnesia comfortably back in place and the whole horrible episode put in a different mind zone. I've told everyone I'm not going to practise walking up and down the catwalk with Sydney – to have to do the whole beastly thing *once* is quite enough, and anyway, I've got too much to do.

The tables and chairs have arrived and are stacked around the gym. Vivi's mother is a florist and she has given us great armfuls of flowers that we have to try to get 'arranged' before the end of the day. We realised last week that we didn't have any vases, so I rang the catering company and, in my best 'pretty please' voice, asked if they might have some we could borrow. They have provided us with six beautiful, big clear cylindrical pots to put the flowers in. We're going to put them on the floor beside the catwalk, three each side, which should look totally fantastic.

Ms Worhause is donating pale pink roses for the tables, which I'm going to put in little beakers from the science lab. Now, is that a brilliant idea or what? Someone's father, I can't remember whose, offered us two trees in pots – those cut-into-amazing-shapes sort of trees, which are standing on either side of the entrance. One of the boys is going through the soundtrack to make sure that the boys on lights faze the spotlights in and out at the right times.

The gym is looking so totally and completely amazing already that the bit of me that ISN'T feeling so sick is feeling really excited.

'Don't forget to take the cheesecakes out of the freezer,' shouts Flossie. We've started the de-frosting and re-crisping process, to get ready for this evening. Now it's time to whizz to Harrods to collect the fresh salad leaves and put the finishing touches to all our hard work.

George pops his head round the door while we're packing up the food and mumbles, 'Hello.'

'Oh, um, hi,' I say back, then I try to see him as possible boyfriend material. It's very difficult, I mean this is GEORGE, good old George who cried when his teddy bear fell into the bath . . . I just don't know what to do about him or what to tell Minnie. He lingers for a few sticky moments, then turns around and leaves. Phew! I'm glad that's over, for the time being.

Mrs Sophie Something-Hyphenated is going to drive me and the food to school in her stinky Range Rover. Thankfully she has to put the seats down to make room, so the icky, sicky children won't fit in (unless of course she puts them in the seats before folding them down . . . squishy, icky children . . .) Flossie and I put everything in plastic boxes for fear of germs (for Portia's benefit) and also because we don't want our beautiful food absorbing the icky, sicky smell from the car.

When we arrive it's action stations all round. Ms Worhause (in peacock blue with red and shocking pink beads) is sailing around the room and has the boys properly organised. They have arranged the tables all around the catwalk, with eight spindly gold chairs at each one. The doors are being blacked out and some boys are trying out the lights and music again. The gorgeous girlies are already there. Minnie has a mouthful of pins and is making last minute adjustments to Vivi's outfit, and Portia and Mercedes are practising their 'turns' on the cat-walk. Mercedes keeps bumping into Portia. She says she's SO nervous. She's worried that she's going to pass out – PANIC! I try hard to calm her down (I really don't want to model *her* dress as well). Then I tune my mind to a different wavelength and I'm quite happy to watch them for a while before asking them to sashay down and help with the tables.

We spread the white cloths and put the glass beakers with pink roses in the middle of each table. Then we lay them all up with the sparkly silver cutlery. Time seems to be passing rather too quickly and we realise we should start to set all the food out in time for the arrival of the first guests. They will have drinks before the show – something that looks like cham-pagne but isn't quite – while the models prepare.

It's time to change into my completely boring black dress and get ready to be the hostess with the mostest. I'm feeling just a teensy bit clammy when the first guests arrive. I even ask someone if I can sew them to a sheet instead of showing them to a seat. But everyone is very nice and they've all dressed to the nines. People seem to be genuinely surprised by how beautiful the gym looks and by the time the guests start eating, my head is swimming with compliments about the food. I feel like prodding Mother and telling her, 'There, you see? Some people think it's really clever to be able to put together a banquet like this!'

George is looking so sweet in his dinner jacket and bow tie. I just know he would be much better off with Minnie than with me. When this is all over I simply *have* to get them together. It might be weird, but not nearly as weird as him and me together.

Things go swimmingly well until suddenly they start playing the music that means I SHOULD BE CHANGING! Oooh, there's that sudden slap-you-in-the-face, cold clammy feeling, when you know you can't pretend any longer that it's not going to happen. Now, I think, if there is a good fairy somewhere up there, she will open the ground up and let me be swallowed whole RIGHT this minute. I close my eyes and wish . . . but no, here I am, still absolutely ALL here and people behind the scenes are beginning to look at me as if they think I should be making a MOVE.

Someone is pushing me towards the changing room. I look around and see Portia and Mercedes looking divine in their wonderful modelly clothes. And then everything goes dark. I just have time to think, 'At last, I've fainted, and not a *minute* too soon,' when I realise that Minnie is pulling my dress off over my head and telling me to 'WAKE UP, Angel! It'll be your turn soon'. I can't seem to move at all as Minnie starts pouring The Dress over my head. I'm going to be SICK. Surely I'm going to throw up . . . if I could be sick right now all over the dress, maybe I wouldn't have to . . .

'Angel, come ON,' squeaks Minnie. 'We have to brush your hair and put your shoes on . . .'

'I can't do this, Minnie,' I whisper in my tiniest voice.

'Of *course* you can do this. Right Angel, you're on next and here comes Sydney . . .'

I just have time to catch sight of someone who resembles me reflected in the mirror, but this person looks tall and glam and is wearing an astonishing dress. Obviously not me. Suddenly there is Sydney – I'd almost forgotten about him in all the horror of having to put this dress on. I look up and realise that I haven't seen Sydney for a few days and for the first time I think that maybe this is awful for him too . . . He's smiling at me, though, and somehow he looks taller than I remember. He's wearing full evening gear, with a black bow tie and a rose in his button-hole and he is actually looking rather ALL RIGHT. Grown-up, even. He grins and says, 'Wow, Angel, you really do look heavenly!' Is he joking again? Oh, what does it matter now that all the shreds of my self-confidence are about to unravel? He seizes my hand and marches me out to the catwalk. Suddenly I can see all the faces. Everyone is there in

was he always this tall?

Sydney

front of me – Mother, Potty, Flossie, George, Diggory, Mrs Sophie Something-Hyphenated, Stinker, lots of Mother's luvvie friends, even Adam. Behind them I can see Ms Worhause smiling . . . but why is everyone looking so gobsmacked? Why is nobody talking or eating or moving or doing anything but staring? Even Mother looks as if she's seen a

golly!!

ghost. Her hand is up to her mouth and I can see her rings glittering in the lights, and Sydney swings me around to face him. He kisses me full on the mouth (ooh, um, he smells delicious) . . . There is a ROAR of applause. I open my eyes, post-kiss, to see Sydney grinning as though grinning was going out of fashion, and as the audience goes on cheering, he says, 'Eat your heart out, Sophie Dahl.' And somehow I just know that *this* time he *isn't* joking!

Street Smart is about safety.
With practical guidelines, tips
for common sense and advice
on how to handle difficult
situations with confidence, it
can help you live your life
safely and independently.
The message is *be aware*,
rather than *beware!* Kerry
Parnell covers the issues
teenagers face, such as:

- drugs and alcohol;
- dating and sex;
- safety on the street and on public transport;
- peer pressure and bullying;
- streetwise know-how – cash machines, pick-pockets,
  strangers;
- internet, email and phone savvy;
- avoiding or coping with abuse, harassment or assault;
- dealing with crime;
- and much more.

By the author of *Bliss - The Smart Girl's Guide to Sex*:
"This accessible and straightforward book . . . provides
facts, reassurance and invaluable advice." *Publishing News*

Sunday 8.00 p.m.
Walking home, I said, "I don't think he's that keen on her. What sort of kiss do you think it was? Was there actual lip contact? Or was it lip to cheek, or lip to corner of mouth?"

"I think it was lip to corner of mouth, but maybe it was lip to cheek?"

"It wasn't **full-frontal snogging** though, was it?"

"No."

"I think she went for full-frontal and he converted it into lip to corner of mouth . . ."

Saturday 6.58 p.m.
Lindsay was wearing a thong! I don't understand **thongs** – what is the point of them? They just go up your bum, as far as I can tell!

Wednesday 10.30 p.m.
Mrs Next Door complained that **Angus** has been frightening their poodle again. He stalks it. I explained, "Well, he's a Scottish wildcat, that's what they do. They stalk their prey. I have tried to train him but he ate his lead."

*"This is very funny – very, very funny. I wish I had read this when I was a teenager, it really is **very funny**."* Alan Davies

'Joseph, are you in there? It's me, your mother.'

Damn, I thought it might be that Jennifer Lopez again; she usually calls round about this time for a quick snog.

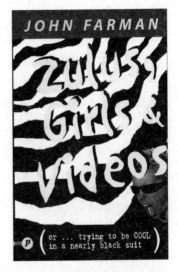

- **ZULUS** I always think my life's a bit like living in that old film *Zulu* – you know, the one where Michael Caine (me) and a bunch of rather hot British soldiers (Rover) are holding this garrison fort in Africa somewhere against thousands of ever-so-cross natives (my family).

- **GIRLS** This is really sad. One minute my head's full of the gorgeous, sexy Jade, and whether I might stand a chance with her after all, and the next, I'm thinking of dear sweet Lucy. Jade–Lucy, Lucy–Jade, I just can't get my brain straight.

- **VIDEOS** I'm a complete cinema junkie – a filmoholic – a movie maniac – a video voyeur, you name it. I don't know why, but all I ever think about is films (oh yes – and girls).

"Lively, witty text by a diverting writer." *Publishing News*

In the same series: *Merlin, Movies and Lucy Something*
Sequins, Stardom and Chloe's Dad

Students have more than ever to learn at school these days, and there seems to be an endless succession of exams and assessments. This book aims to help you not only to master the skills of concentration, but also to relax. It may even help you to enjoy your studies!

Learn how to:

- get organised, work to a routine, yet be flexible and adaptable;
- work in your preferred learning style and with the eight forms of intelligence;
- recognise and overcome the limits you put on yourself;
- avoid the effects of dehydration, lack of oxygen and caffeine sensitivity;
- get into 'The Flow';
- and much, much more . . .

By the author of *Smart Thinking*:
"It's an engaging, clear and positive exploration of the nature of self-belief. Well worth making available – and reading yourself." *The Guardian*

I flopped on the beanbag next to her. I felt happy. Iz and me. Me and Iz talking about stuff and Iz predicting my future.

'What does it say, Madam Rose?'

'Oh interesting,' Iz murmured. 'Very interesting. The card that crosses you is the Wheel of Fortune. It signifies a new chapter. A turning point.'

But a turning point is exactly what Lucy does NOT want. Everything is changing around her, and suddenly she is required to make all sorts of decisions.

- Everyone else knows who and what they want to be except her.
- Izzie has become friends with the glamorous Nesta and Lucy isn't certain she likes this new threesome.
- Nesta and Izzie look sixteen, but Lucy, at fourteen, can easily pass for a twelve-year-old.

But the day Lucy sees the most wonderful boy crossing the street, things do start to change – in all areas of her life . . .

By the same author: *Mates, Dates and Sole Survivors*
White Lies and Barefaced Truths